THE GLASS CEILING

THE GLASS CEILING

Anabel Donald

G.K. Hall & Co. • Chivers Press
Thorndike, Maine USA   Bath, Avon, England

This Large Print edition is published by G.K. Hall & Co., USA and by Chivers Press, England.

Published in 1995 in the U.S. by arrangement with St. Martin's Press, Inc.

Published in 1995 in the U.K. by arrangement with Macmillan London Limited.

U.S. Softcover	0-7838-1522-0	(Paperback Collection Edition)
U.K. Hardcover	0-7451-3899-3	(Chivers Large Print)
U.K. Softcover	0-7451-3900-0	(Camden Large Print)

G.K. Hall Large Print Paperback Collection.

The text of this Large Print edition is unabridged.
Other aspects of the book may vary from the original edition.

Set in 16 pt. News Plantin by Rick Gundberg.

Printed in the United States on permanent paper.

British Library Cataloguing in Publication Data available

Library of Congress Cataloging in Publication Data

Donald, Anabel.
    The glass ceiling / Anabel Donald.
       p.   cm.
    ISBN 0-7838-1522-0 (lg. print : lsc)
    1. Women in television broadcasting — Fiction. 2. Large type books. I. Title.
    [PR6054.O4587G58   1995b]
    823'.914—dc20
                                                    95-36081

For Freddy Stockwell

a remarkable father who has taught me nearly everything I know. And never mentioned a glass ceiling.

Sunday, 26 September

Chapter 1

I don't like formal upper-class English manners, and not just because I don't have them. 'Lovely, darling, wonderful, darling, thank you sooo much,' and all the time, underneath, what they really think. It makes me feel patronised.

On the other hand . . . manners can come in useful. Sometimes. For example, if you've just had one of the least successful sexual experiences of all time, with a man you particularly want to succeed with. Times like that.

There we were. In bed, at Barty's place. Two wineglasses on two bedside tables. An empty bottle of Château Pointlessly Expensive, his side. A dazed-looking cheese-plant my side, its waxy leaves reeling under the impact of my wine, which I had been too cautious to drink. I didn't want to make a fool of myself, did I?

Big mistake. I should have.

I should have drunk the wine and relaxed.

Failing that, I should have faked it; sounded pleased, moved, thrilled. Shaken to my depths. Every woman's done it, some time. I certainly have. I'm twenty-nine years old, and reasonably experienced. There's always plenty of spare about if you work in television, particularly if you're on location, and when I started out (probably

9

because I had low physical self-esteem and a high sex-drive) I seldom said no. I'd developed two styles, over the years. I could have given him kittenish purrings culminating in the piercing scream of a pre-teen at a Michael Jackson concert, or the simpler, all-purpose 'Mmm. Mmmmm. Mmmmm . . . Oh, God!'

But I hadn't. I'd lain there hoping to be excited and tried to be co-operative, like a friend helping to hang a picture straight. Up a bit, down a bit, to the right a bit, no, not quite, try that, so now here we were after an hour of nothing very much, staring at a moulded ceiling pooled in the overlapping beams of two Art Deco bedside lamps. I clutched the duvet under my chin and refused to imagine losing Barty.

He's an independent producer I work with, and in the last few tax years he's provided over 60 per cent of my freelance income as a researcher. We've had a will-they-won't-they relationship for a while now, partly because I wouldn't risk mixing business with pleasure.

I'd been right.

One of the things about him that usually annoys me is his smoothness. But now I was counting on it. I wasn't going to risk speaking first: I waited for clues from his dog-eared copy of the Bullshit Manual for old Etonians.

'Very dear Alex,' he said. 'You're more important to me than you can imagine. Didn't you say you had an appointment at ten o'clock? It's a quarter to ten now.'

Got it. Simple. Say something positive but vague, then go and let the dust settle on our sexual egos. 'You're important to me too,' I said, and got out of bed.

'Shall I drive you?'

'No, I'll enjoy the walk,' I said, and bolted. Pulled on my jeans, T-shirt and Doc Martens, stuffed my pants, bra and socks in my big squashy leather bag, babbled about my appointment, and went like a whippet for the stairs. I didn't even say thank you for the wine. The cheese-plant could do that.

Out in the street I gulped in the London air. Another big mistake. Humid, toxic September air. I coughed for a while. The crucial thing was not to think. I covered my ears with my hands to block out the sneering voices inside my head, and said, 'Rhubarb rhubarb rhubarb rhubarb.'

Then I looked at my watch. No watch. It was on the bedside table. I wasn't going back. I was going to meet a client. Work. Work always helps.

By ten o'clock I'd half walked, half jogged the three-quarters of a mile up Ladbroke Grove, and I was standing under Westway, not far from my flat. Only about three streets away, but three significant streets: a headlong plunge down the urban scale, from marginally smart to inner-city deprived.

It hadn't rained for two days, but the huge dank concrete flyover above my head was still mustering greasy drops of London water (I hoped

11

it was water), which were splatting at my feet. The traffic, only a few yards above me, was a constant rumbling roar that almost blanketed the voices from the takeaway West Indian food van on Ladbroke Grove.

The Barty fiasco was bad enough. But even without it, standing here, I would have felt embarrassed, an intruder. The darker parts under Westway belong to the winos at night. Not the young homeless, on their way up to rescue at a Young People's Drop-in Centre or down to a brief blaze of glory as sex objects followed by a dragging decline as drug addicts, but real, dyed-in-the-wool tramps, with their rotting filthy garments and bulging plastic bags and bottles of Thunderbird or cans of Special Brew. I was trespassing in someone's front room. Or someone's urinal. One muttering old wreck passed and accosted me.

'Gissa quid for a cuppa tea.'

I gave her a quid.

She spat. 'Can't get much tea for that. Costa livin'.'

I added another quid. She took it, spat again and moved on, pushing a clanking pram.

It was five past ten. It had started to rain heavily, but at least I knew that was water. I'd wait for the Woman in the Balaclava Helmet until quarter past, and then go home.

I didn't think she was going to turn up. So far, she was only a voice on my answerphone, and I'd had some odd calls since I put up an advertisement locally.

On balance, I'd regretted it. Not advertising: if you don't advertise, you can't get hired, and I was still trying to get my sideline, private detective work, off the ground. The location of the ad wasn't bad either: in my neighbourhood sub-post office, just by where people stood in queues for hours for Child Benefit or pensions or stamps. They had plenty of time to look up at the signs, read them, set them to music, make anagrams out of them. Beside the Indian takeaway and the dodgy garage and the spaces saying 'This space is available for advertising', my ad looked tempting. It had my address and telephone number, and,

ALEX TANNER
PRIVATE INVESTIGATOR
SPECIAL RATES FOR INTERESTING
CASES

The mistake was in the choice of the word 'interesting'. Everyone thinks they're an interesting case. Particularly the lunatics, and you get plenty of those in my corner of London. The advertisement had been up three weeks, and so far I'd got two real jobs out of it. One lasted half a day: the other, two days. Apart from that, I'd had telephone calls from several nutters, and the Woman in the Balaclava Helmet was probably another of them.

The trouble with answerphones is that you can't argue.

13

The message had been waiting that morning, early, when I got in from my run. About eight o'clock. I'd played it back often enough. I knew it by heart. I'd even put a new tape on the answering machine so I could keep the original message safe.

'Alex Tanner? Private Investigator? I'm a client. Call me Ms X. I want to hire you. Meet me outside the Westway Senior Citizens' Centre at ten o'clock tonight. I'll be wearing a Balaclava helmet.'

The voice had an Irish accent, but it was clearly put on. And not professionally, either. It moved hokily from Belfast to Dublin to Cork and back again. So the accent was assumed, and all I really knew was that it belonged to a woman, and not a very young or very old woman. A woman who wasn't Irish or of Irish origin, with a moderate ear for accents, between the ages of eighteen and fifty-five. That really narrowed it down.

Did I even expect her to turn up? Yes, I did. Or perhaps I just hoped she would. I like mysteries, fictional or real. I always have. Problem. Inquiry. Investigation. Audacity. Solution. Everything sorted by the last page. I don't have any real-life heroes, but I have fictional ones. Like Philip Marlowe and Lew Archer and Spenser. Private eyes who walk the mean streets wearing the shining armour of a visionary cynicism, Arthurian knights out of time, where Avalon meets the streets of Los Angeles or Bay City. And a Woman in a Balaclava Helmet suggested a latterday Avalon.

But by ten-thirty, when I'd fended off two more winos, I had to admit there was no sign of the Holy Grail and my armour was soaked through. So I walked south up Ladbroke Grove for the three hundred yards that spanned the huge social gap between the winos and my property investment. I was going home, to Peter.

Usually, I live alone and that's the way I like it. I very seldom have guests. Guests, female, sleep when I want to hoover and hoover when I want to sleep. Guests, male, make me self-conscious. If they're current lovers they should know me well enough not to stay. Otherwise I can't walk about in the early morning as I usually do, with no clothes on, but have to behave like someone in a seventies movie who can't get out of bed without trussing herself up in a king-size sheet and trailing it across the grubby carpet.

Not that my flat's dirty: it isn't. If anything, I clean rather too much. It's just that I live in London, where carpets and curtains go from new to grubby before the cheque that you bought them with clears.

But I'd agreed to let Peter stay, for several good reasons.

He was an ex-lover, so he knew the worst. I didn't need to impress him.

He'd offered to put up bookshelves in my spare room, free.

I wanted to keep in with his father, who was my best contact in the Metropolitan Police.

So when I got back to my flat, instead of walking

15

into a people-free sanctuary, burying my face in a pillow and howling with the embarrassment of it all, I was going to have to be social.

My flat's the top two floors of the building. As I reached the top of the communal stairs I could hear the television, and Peter. 'Get in there!' he was shouting. 'Rip his balls off!'

A once-familiar domestic sound: Peter watching a rugby match. He'd been working on a documentary in Alaska for five months: he'd asked me to record the British Lions tour of Australia and New Zealand for him. Which I had, and was suffering through it. 'You left-footed twat, my grandmother could have converted from there! Oh, hi, Alex.' He snapped off the video.

He was lying on the sofa, his big feet in their desert boots hanging off the end, pointedly. I'd bet he'd just moved his feet when he heard my key in the lock. I'm the only person allowed to put their boots up on my sofa, and he knows it.

The living-room looked smaller with him in it. He's not all that tall — about five-eight — but he's broad and well-built and he has a big head with masses of curly chestnut hair and a redder beard. I hoped the beard wouldn't be with us much longer; he'd grown it in Alaska, probably for warmth or convenience.

'Client didn't turn up?' he said. He'd predicted she wouldn't. I shook my head. 'Never mind,' he said. 'There's a parcel for you. Someone rang the doorbell and left it on the steps.'

16

He waved a brown muscular arm towards the kitchen. 'I left it on the table,' he said. 'Fetch us a beer, while you're at it.'

'We're out of beer.'

'No. I stocked up. Coors. In the fridge.'

I like Coors, but it's a luxury I won't waste my own money on. He was being nice to me. He usually is: he likes women, and he likes me. We've known each other since I was eight and he was nine and he let me join his gang. He'd lived with his family on the same council estate in Fulham I'd partly grown up in.

Come to that, I'm fond of him. I've almost forgiven him for dumping me for the blonde graduate BBC trainee, and that was ten years ago. Ten years rubs the edges off even the most catastrophic deprivation, and I'd seen it as that at the time. It had knocked my sexual confidence.

About most things, I'm confident. Partly because I'm good at my job. Certainly good at my main job, and not so bad at my PI sideline, either. But I never expect to be desired, or loved. I always used to suppose most other people did. They certainly give that impression. Recently, I haven't been so sure.

Anyway, I didn't moan at him about lying on the sofa, and went upstairs. I washed, changed into clean underclothes, dry jeans and sweatshirt. Then I fished the dirty underclothes from my bag and stuffed them into the laundry basket, put the lid firmly on the basket and stray memories of Barty's bedroom, and left my boots dripping in the bath. Then I fetched two bottles of beer, some rubber gloves and the parcel, and sat in the armchair, leaving the sofa to him.

I'd handled the parcel carefully, wrapping the rubber gloves round it, and I put them on before I opened it, so as not to smudge the fingerprints, supposing there were any, supposing it mattered. The parcel was actually a large envelope addressed to ALEX TANNER, FLAT 2, in large print. There was a cardboard box inside, about eight inches by four by four. The box was fastened shut with Sellotape all the way round.

I like small puzzles. I hefted the box in my hand before I opened it. It didn't rattle. It wasn't heavy, it wasn't light.

I took a swig of the beer, put the can down on an old envelope to protect the surface of my coffee table, and started to slit the Sellotape with a key.

'What is it?' said Peter.

I lifted the lid off and nearly dropped the box. I'm not squeamish, particularly, but the beady eyes of the hamster met mine, or didn't meet mine because his/hers were glazed and definitely dead. Dead things are frightening. Even small dead things, when you don't expect them.

'A hamster,' I said.

'Yer what?' said Peter, heaving himself round so he could see for himself.

'A dead hamster,' I repeated. It looked pathetic, defenceless, its small pink paws curling appealingly.

'What did it die of?'

'Maybe it was bored to death by a one-eyed Haitian serial hamster killer singing highlights from the musicals of Andrew Lloyd Webber. How do I know?'

'Is it injured?'

'No, it's dead. Passed on. Passed over. Gone to Jesus. Gone to the Big Wheel in the Sky.'

'A know that,' said Peter impatiently. 'But is it damaged? Tortured?'

'No.' Its coat was smooth and rather beautiful.

I went to the kitchen for a plastic bag. OK, it was only a hamster, but it was dead and that was worrying. Death is always worrying. I lifted it on to the plastic bag, not wincing at the contact of its soft coat because the rubber gloves blunted that. I can bear most things through rubber gloves.

At the bottom of the box was an envelope. Inside, two hundred pounds in fifty-pound notes, and a letter. Not hand-written: produced by a dot-matrix printer.

Alex Tanner
I am your client, the Womun in the Balaclava Helmet. I know what Wimmin really want.

Leona Power XXX
Melanie Slater
Elspeth Driscoll
Grace Macarthy
I must smash the glass ceiling. Stop me if

you can . . . please stop me.

I held the note out to Peter, not letting him take it (fingerprints again). He read it, slowly, which is how he reads. 'She can't spell,' he said. 'She's spelt "woman" wrong. Twice.'

'That's the feminist spelling. *Womun* singular, *wimmin* plural.'

'She's a nutcase, then.'

I was annoyed. 'Because she's a feminist?'

'Not just, though that too, I suppose. Mostly because she makes an appointment which she doesn't keep and sends you a dead hamster.'

I wasn't going to waste time arguing feminism with Peter. He's hopeless. Not only is he an amateur rugby player, but he's also a television technician, a breed which has a canteen culture only marginally less primitive and 'get out your danglers, darlin' ' than the police.

He read the note again. 'Leona Power I know. She's the good-looking American feminist with tasty legs and big tits. Everyone knows Amazin' Grace Macarthy, New Zealand's answer to Germaine Greer. Who are the other two?'

'Melanie Slater's a Tory tabloid columnist. She used to be feminist and left-wing — ages ago. Then she saw the light, and now she's all for Family Values and putting single parents in the workhouse. I interviewed her two years ago for a doco on Getting Women Back Into the Kitchen.'

'What's a workhouse?'

'Never mind.' I'd forgotten that Peter's idea

20

of history was an early Beatles album. 'I've never heard of Elspeth Driscoll . . . It doesn't even ring a bell.'

'If you've met the Slater woman, maybe she sent this. Did you tell her you were a PI on the side?'

'No. I wasn't, then. And she wouldn't have hired me anyway. I'm not her type, I told you. She thinks women should have hairstyles, high heels and husbands. Not cropped hair, DMs and career plans.'

Peter sat up, concentrating. 'So this Slater woman was a feminist once?'

'Yeah.'

'So it looks as if this is a list of feminists? That's what Power and Macarthy are.'

'Yeah.'

'Why the crosses after Leona Power?'

I could hardly believe he didn't know. But, come to that, there aren't too many news bulletins in a hut in Alaska. 'Because she's dead,' I said. 'She died last month.'

Chapter 2

Peter was interested. 'Do you think this woman killed her?'

'I don't see how she can have. It was a car accident, one of those flukes. She was driving on a country road on her way back to London from some place in the sticks, and a driver coming the other way had a heart attack, lost control and hit her head-on. As far as I remember from the inquest.'

I'd probably got it right: facts are my business and I have a fly-paper memory.

'But if she doesn't mean she's killed her, what does she mean, *Stop me if you can?*'

'I don't know, Peter,' I said rather crossly. 'How should I know?'

'You know most things,' he said. 'Or claim to.'

'Stop bitching . . . Watch the rugby.'

'This accident, it sounds like an act of God, right? Like you're walking along and an engine falls off an aeroplane and lands on your head.'

'Sort of.'

'So nobody could have fixed it except God. Maybe she thinks she's God. Just like I said, a nutter.'

We both looked at the hamster.

'Or maybe the crosses mean something else,' I said. 'What time is it?'

'Quarter to eleven.'

'Pass me the telephone.' I needed to know who Elspeth Driscoll was, and if she was a feminist of any kind my old mate Jordan would know. It wasn't too late to ring her: she seldom went to bed before three in the morning.

When Jordan answered, I identified myself then held the receiver away from my ear. She always coughed, but she coughed longest on the telephone, on other people's time. I'd noticed a while back that when she rang me, which was seldom — I often needed her information; she seldom needed mine, and though she was gay she didn't fancy me — she coughed much less.

When the spasm was over, there was a silence. She'd gone to fetch her cigarettes, her lighter and an ashtray. I waited till she'd sat down again and lit up. I was lucky she hadn't changed the music on the CD player and cooked a four-course meal while she was at it.

Peter watched me in astonishment. 'Who're you calling?' he said.

'Jordan.'

'You're with a man,' the receiver quacked accusingly.

'Not a man. Only Peter,' I said. 'My long-ago cameraman. A friendly blast from the past. Listen, Jordan, who's Elspeth Driscoll?'

She coughed again. 'How much detail do you want?'

23

'Anything you have.'

'I've got her phone number. I called for a comment three weeks ago, when I was doing a tribute to Leona Power for the *Guardian*. If you need any more, you'll have to find it yourself. She hasn't done anything that I can remember since . . . oh, the early seventies.'

'What did she do then?'

'She was still one of the Vestal Virgins. At Oxford. It was a pioneering women's group, for England. They were much further ahead in the States, of course. It was led by Macarthy and Power.'

'Was Melanie Slater a Vestal Virgin?'

'Yes, she was,' snapped Jordan, who is very competitive about information. 'If you know so much about it, why are you asking me?'

'I'm asking you because you know everything about women's movements and I know very little,' I said, 'and that's all the grovelling you'll get, so take it and like it. Tell me about the Vestal Virgins.'

'Power and Macarthy were the co-founders. They were a bit older than the others, because though they were undergraduates they'd both already taken degrees in their own countries, Power in America — Vassar, I think — and Macarthy in New Zealand. They were in Oxford on scholarships, and had a lot more savvy than the other two, Slater and Driscoll. And a lot more brains.'

She coughed, spluttered, and left the phone.

I put the receiver down, drained my beer, and

went to the kitchen to fetch two more. When I came back the receiver was quacking. 'Tanner? Tanner? Get your buns back here. Now.'

'I'm here,' I said mildly. 'I needed more beer.' I passed one to Peter.

'Did you see my *Guardian* piece?'

'No.'

'It has a quote from Driscoll. And a photograph. The Vestal Virgins in a punt on the Isis, 1969. Weren't we all young and beautiful then?'

I'd been five. Jordan must have been in her late thirties: she was well past sixty now, and looked like a hyperactive monkey, brown and thin and shrivelled and jerky. I try never to alienate a contact, however. 'Yes,' I said nostalgically. 'Those were the days.'

'Starring in "Show and Tell" at nursery school, were you?' she said sarkily. I like that about Jordan. She's an unguided missile: you never know where she'll come at you from. Flattering her is a challenge. 'D'you want me to fax it through now?'

'Yes, do that. And give me her telephone number, would you? And Macarthy's? I've got Melanie Slater's.'

'I don't have them to hand. Tomorrow morning do you?'

'Tonight would be better.'

'Not for me. You've interrupted a love tryst, and I'm getting right back to it when I've finished this ciggy. You'll get it tomorrow morning and like it.'

'I'll like it.'

'Are you going to tell me why you want to know?'

'Not right now. I wouldn't want to hold up the course of true love, would I? What's she like?'

'Young, gorgeous and dim as the lighting in a New York bar. Talk to you soon. Hey — I've just remembered something else about Driscoll. D'you want it?'

'Please.'

'She wrote a book. A feminist book. Published in the mid-eighties. Total crap. Grace tried to drum up some kind of reviewing for it but it died the death. 'Bye.'

She hung up on her cough: I hung up too, and waited until the article inched and clicked its way out of the fax. It was more than A4 size: Jordan had had to cut it up. The photographs came first. A familiar picture of Leona Power, a studio one which she'd been using for publicity for the last two years or so, because I remembered it from displays in booksellers' windows. It was backlit and flattering, but she didn't need much flattering anyway. She'd had a beautiful face, fine-boned and delicate, and it had aged well. Like many Americans, she inhabited the timewarp Skilful Beauty Care: it could have been her in her early thirties. Her blonde hair still looked alive and young. Good hairdressers, good make-up. She'd never neglected appearances. She'd thought they were important, and for her they had been. I'd read some of her work and it was mostly collections of what other people thought and said.

Not a great original thinker, Leona Power, but she could always be relied on to look pretty and smile.

The photograph I really wanted came through next. The Vestal Virgins in their punt. Four young faces, four young women in tiny late-sixties skirts, all legs. Grace Macarthy's legs dominated the photograph, partly because they were so long, partly because she was the only one standing up, because she was poling the punt. She was a very tall woman, with a handsome face, hawklike rather than puddingy, despite her youth. She had plenty of thick straight sixties hair and her eyes looked straight into the camera. The others were posing. She wasn't. She was impatient and she held her punt-pole like an offensive weapon.

Peter'd got up from the sofa and was looking over my shoulder. 'She's a knockout,' he said.

'Which one?' McCarthy was magnificent; the other three all looked similar to me, pretty, forgettable, young.

'That one.' He pointed to a girl in the front of the picture. She had very short hair, large eyes, a little pointed chin. According to the caption under the photo it was Elspeth Driscoll. You couldn't tell from looking at her then what she'd look like now.

And I'd never have recognized any of the three kittenish child/women of the picture in the hard-faced Melanie 'Shoot Single Mothers' Slater I'd interviewed. Not for a moment.

'Alex, where's this glass ceiling, then?' said

Peter. He was back at the letter again.

'It's not a thing or a place, it's a feminist idea,' I said. 'It's the invisible barrier men put up to stop women being really successful — rising to be High Court judges or top bankers or chairmen of international companies or consultants in top hospitals or —'

'Yeah, yeah, I get the point. But some of them are.'

'Not nearly enough.'

'All that stuff's out of date. Everything's changed. I had a female sound recordist working with me last year, for Chrissake. She was a real dog. Built like a brick shithouse.'

'Was she a good sound recordist?'

'All right. No, be fair, she was good. But she looked like hell.'

I took a deep breath. Some time when we were on location together for a month I'd raise his consciousness. Maybe.

He went on. 'So this sounds like paranoid bull-shit to me.'

'Paranoid cowshit, perhaps. I don't agree. I think there is a glass ceiling, but right now I'm more interested in how the Womun plans to smash it. I can't see that killing feminists will help.'

'You say the Melanie Slater woman is anti-feminist? Killing her might.'

'But why Grace Macarthy? None of it makes sense,' I said.

'So what're you going to do about it, then?' said Peter, his eyes pulling back to the television.

28

He wanted to watch the rest of the rugby video, I could see, and I didn't mind: he was more hindrance than help, anyway.

'I'm going to work a day for the Womun in the Balaclava Helmet,' I said. 'Nutcase or not, she's paid for it. After that . . . we'll see.'

Monday, 27 September

Chapter 3

I didn't sleep, of course. Not much. Not with having someone else in the flat with me. Peter didn't go to bed until two and then the silence was even more disturbing than the rugby had been. I worked my way through two early Dick Francises (would I have been any better in bed with Sid Halley? Probably, he was crippled) and fell asleep trying not to think about Barty. Our bedroom catastrophe hadn't been his fault, I knew. He'd done all the right things: it was just that he'd been trying to do them to me, and I'd been terrified. Or anxious. Or embarrassed. Or self-conscious. Or all the above. Maybe, I kept thinking, maybe I was condemned to a series of relationships that were only successful if I didn't respect the person I was having a relationship with.

I got up at seven, after two hours' sleep, and went for a run around Wormwood Scrubs. After a mile I felt better. When you run you don't think, you ruminate, and embarrassment goes away with the pumping of your legs and the blood thumping in your ears. I started ruminating about the Womun's letter and what she meant by *I know what Wimmin really want.* The question was originally Freud's, I thought, and he hadn't come up with an answer. Wisely, in my view. It was a silly question: too general, and possibly reflecting no more than his own neurotic need for control.

And how, exactly, did she intend to smash the glass ceiling?

Running, I'd also forgotten Peter. When I got back, luckily, he was still asleep in the tiny spare bedroom off my living-room. His snores filled the flat. I had a bath, then retreated into the kitchen, closed the door behind me, put the radio on — Classic FM — and did the washing-up while I was waiting for the coffee to perk. I had to decide how best to deploy a day's work for my no-show hamster-sending client.

My morning was almost full already: I had an appointment at nine-thirty and another at twelve. I also had a back-log of paperwork to clear. Until three months ago, I'd never let the paperwork pile up. Then I'd acquired a temporary assistant, Claudia. Not an employee: I couldn't afford one. A rich kid who paid me to train her. After a while she'd been useful and I got to rely on her. Last week Claudia'd left for Paris and a year's training course at a media school (a fill-in before she went to Harvard) and all the word-processing and filing she would have done was silting up my desk in the living-room.

That would have to wait. So would the Womun in the Balaclava Helmet, at least till the afternoon, by which time Jordan should have faxed me the telephone numbers of Macarthy and Driscoll. So would the hamster, which was lying in a plastic bag on the second shelf of my fridge.

When I left the flat at nine Peter was still asleep. I propped a note on the telephone: *Out at least until early afternoon.* That would give him a chance to watch rugby in the morning and get out of the flat for the rest of the day. I hoped. I was almost out of the door when I remembered his appetite and his just-woken lack of grip and went back to add a PS to my note: *Dead hamster in fridge. Do not eat.*

My first appointment wasn't likely to be profitable. I'd wriggled for two weeks to get out of it, ignoring the messages Claudia kept passing on, and then the messages left on the answerphone, but finally Mary's insistent voice whining 'Please call back, Alex' wore me down. She thought I owed her. She'd been my social worker since I was four, when the Social Services first tumbled to the fact that I was living in an unheated, filthy flat with a woman (my mother) who was well out of her head most of the time and who conducted her life according to instructions given by the Voices of Clark Gable and the Pope, neither of whom seemed to know much about child nutrition.

After that Mary moved my mother in and out of mental hospitals and me in and out of foster homes. None of her efforts had been particularly successful but she had tried, she'd never given up, she'd always been there for me. Or so she repeatedly said, though I'd never wanted her *there*. Wherever that was.

We'd parted company when I turned eighteen and could officially look after myself, and I hadn't seen her since, though she'd rung occasionally, particularly at the beginning, and still sent me birthday cards. Now she wanted me to meet her in a coffee-shop in Queensway at nine-thirty. 'I need your help,' she'd said.

She'd spent fourteen years *being there* for me. Now I'd spend thirty minutes in a coffee-shop for her. The least I could do, I suppose.

I was early to the meet — I'd walked, and over-estimated how long it would take — but she was earlier. She sat at a small table by the window of the half-empty Austrian coffee-shop, sorting through a sheaf of documents, occasionally making notes. Just outside the window, Queensway was crowded. A mixed neighbourhood: cosmopolitan, half-rootless, many of the residents transient Arabs or Turks or middle-Europeans with a ballast of well-off English, still in September topped up with end-of-summer tourists shopping till they dropped. It was a cool, blue-sky day, with a bright but heat-free sun, and before I went in to Mary I lingered on the pavement admiring the range of languages represented in the foreign newspapers rack outside the next-door newsagent.

I don't pray. Who's to pray to? But if I'd been a believer I'd have been thanking God to be twenty-nine and healthy and self-employed and independent and in London. And I hadn't thought about Barty once since my run . . . although I was now, of course.

I pushed him aside with the door to the coffee-shop, and went in.

Mary must by now be in her early fifties but she doesn't look it. She's one of those narrow women with dark straight greasy shoulder-length hair and sallow acne skin who look thirty-five when they're twenty and don't abandon that position till they're old. She'd always looked tired; she looked tired now, and she was bundled up against the cold in layers of beige/brown/paprika garments which had probably been produced by tribal collectives in the Third World.

We got through the 'how was I' and 'what had I been doing' and 'did I want a cake with my coffee' (I did: I never pass up free food) in double-quick time because the pattern of our relationship had been set early on: she talked, I listened. When I was a child I'd thought it was because she was an egomaniac. Now, relaxing a little, I realized she'd probably done it to set me at my ease. While we waited for the coffee and cakes she told me what she'd done in the eleven years since we'd last met.

Career-wise, she'd kept rising, and was now high up in the Social Services hierarchy; that's why, I supposed, she could afford her clothes, which although unattractive would probably not have been cheap. Her emotional life was less successful. Oliver, her live-in lover, had left her to explore his sexuality and set up house with a male West Indian probation officer. However, Mary now had three cats and a tidy flat and was considering a Ph.D. course with the Open University.

I nodded supportively whenever she paused, helped the waitress wedge the cups and plates on to our tiny round fake marble table, and waited for Mary to come to the point. Finally, she did. 'I want you to provide a work-experience placement for one of my clients,' she said.

The word 'client' had always got up my nose. I'd never been a client; I'd been a victim or a child at risk or a pain in the butt. Mum had never been a client either. She'd been a mental patient or an incompetent mother or an unlucky human being. But in Mary's jargon we'd only been clients. She probably thought of her acne as a dermatological challenge.

'Tell me about the client,' I said.

'Nick Straker's her name. Seventeen, in care, placed with foster parents, just beginning her second year at a sixth-form college doing four A Levels.'

'If she's just beginning the academic year, why's she doing work experience now?'

'She isn't attending college regularly.'

'Is she attending at all?'

'No.'

'Can't she keep up with the lessons?'

'She's well ahead in all her subjects. She got full marks in her summer examinations.'

I whistled. Full marks. That meant science/ maths, I supposed, but it also meant she was bright. Maybe very bright. 'What is she doing with herself, then? Staying in bed?'

'Not exactly. She isn't going home either. She doesn't find her foster parents very — congenial. It's a pity. They're a very stable, caring, politically sound family.'

'So what *is* she doing?'

'Sleeping rough round Paddington, and — er —"

'Working the streets?'

'No. Working in libraries.'

Pause. Mary looked at me with what would have been an appealing gaze if she'd had a better skin. As it was it came out as the 'before' shot of a skin lotion ad. 'She's a one-off, Alex. Like you were. Give her a hand. For old times' sake.'

I didn't think Mary and I had had the sort of old times that you did things for the sake of. I thought our old times had been the kind that you bolt from, and keep running. But Nick Straker sounded OK to me, and I'd got used to an assistant. 'You realize I work as a private investigator, some of the time?' I said.

'Yes. Your assistant Claudia told me. Nice girl.'

'She is . . . I wouldn't have to pay a salary? Or a National Insurance stamp?'

'No, and I've arranged for a small grant from the Emergency Fund for expenses, and for insurance to cover your employer's liability. I've brought the forms for you to sign.'

'Have you told Nick about it? What does she think?'

'She didn't object . . . I've brought a summary of her file. What I think you should know.'

'Has she attempted suicide?'

'No.'

'Ever been violent?'

'No. Some minor self-mutilation . . .'

'Does she use drugs?'

'Not as far as I know.'

'You needn't give me her file, then. She'll tell me what I need to know.'

Mary hesitated. 'I don't think so,' she said finally.

'Why not?'

'She doesn't actually — communicate easily. She finds it a challenge to — express herself.'

Mary was guilty. She'd retreated into empathy-speak. I washed down my last mouthful of cream cake with a gulp of coffee. 'Cut the crap, Mary. Does she talk?'

'Well — no.'

'Since when?'

'There's — some confusion about that. We think she may talk to her peers, occasionally, and to people on the street. She supports herself by begging. There's nothing organically wrong with her. She spoke normally until two years ago.'

'What happened two years ago to silence her?'

'Her mother died. She was taken into care.'

Mary was watching me anxiously, waiting for me to turn Nick down. I wasn't going to. Claudia had talked non-stop; a silent assistant would be a welcome change, and it was only two weeks, after all. And Mary had tried, with me. She was a trier. You have to acknowledge them, even if they're wrong-headed, even if, I realized with insight I didn't particularly relish, their trying only earns them contempt because the objects of their efforts resent them.

Maybe I'd misjudged Mary. Maybe she was an honest, good-hearted, competent woman who spent her life shovelling other people's shit. And maybe she'd done a good job on me, even though I liked to think I'd done it all myself.

Well, now she was handing me a spade; last chance not to take it. Say no, Alex. Do the sensible thing.

'Where is she now?' I said.

'Waiting for us in McDonald's, up the road.'

Chapter 4

Nick was tallish — about five-eight — with narrow hips, a flat chest and long legs, as far as I could see under her layers of sleeping-rough clothes. She was probably half-Chinese: her hair was very dark and straight, what was left of it. One of her minor self-mutilations was hair-cutting, or tugging, or both. Most of the top of her scalp was bare, but the lower fringe that she'd overlooked or was saving for a rainy day said 'Asian'. So did her long, narrow, opaque, inexpressive eyes. Her skin was pale and her features nondescript apart from a long slightly squashed-looking nose. She carried with her four bulging plastic bags and a powerful smell.

We walked home from the Queensway McDonald's in silence. I hadn't looked back, but I'd have bet Mary watched us anxiously until we were out of sight. I hadn't offered to help Nick with her bags and they were clearly heavy, but she walked vigorously, and easily kept up with me. She didn't talk; I didn't talk. I was thinking. I don't know what she was doing.

By the time we reached the flat I'd replanned the day to incorporate an assistant. Peter was on the sofa, watching the rugby, yelling. They were enthusiastic yells. Perhaps this was a match the Lions won. He made a gesture towards the remote control, but I said, 'Keep watching. Nick, Peter. Peter, Nick. Nick's my new assistant.'

'Hi,' said Peter, his eyes flicking over her, his nostrils involuntarily flaring at the smell. She didn't look back at him: odd. Most women did. It wasn't just his body, though that was well above average. It was probably his eyes. They're an unusual cream sherry colour and they look alert, amused and responsive.

I took her through to the kitchen. 'The bathroom's upstairs,' I said. 'Take a towel from the airing cupboard. Washing-machine over there. D'you have any clean clothes?'

She shook her head.

'OK, I'll find you some. Jeans and a sweatshirt do you?'

She nodded.

'What's your bra size?'

She put down the bags, fished a notebook and pencil from the pocket of her long black Oxfam-shop cardigan, and wrote *I don't wear one, usually.*

She could spell 'usually'. She could punctuate. And she went upstairs to run a bath, so she could take a hint. Nearly my dream employee.

I went downstairs to my friend Polly's flat to get the gear for Nick. Polly's about her height — taller than me — and she wouldn't mind me raiding her cupboards. Besides, she was away in Hong Kong for three months, so she wouldn't know.

When I got back with a pair of Naf-Naf jeans

43

and a black sweatshirt, Nick was sitting on a chair in the living-room shrouded in a towel, and Peter's eyes were flicking between the television screen and what he could see of her legs. 'Don't even think about it,' I said. He waved his left hand in a mock salute and Nick vanished upstairs. I followed her, gave her Polly's clothes and some pants and socks of mine, and said, 'Have you put your clothes in to wash?'

She nodded.

'OK. See you downstairs in a bit.'

The living-room was quiet, the television blank. Peter was crashing about in the kitchen.

I hoped he'd stay there for as long as it took me to listen to the two messages on the answering machine. The first, from Jordan, I fast-forwarded. Nick could transcribe it later. The second was from Barty. When I heard his voice I switched it off. I couldn't bear to listen. But I couldn't bear not to listen either . . . I switched it on again.

'Hello, Alex. I've got your watch. Let's meet. Give me a call.'

Winner of the Noncommittal Prize. I'd call him later. Maybe.

I wasn't going to miss my twelve o'clock appointment, because it looked like money. It was with a solicitor, in a brasserie off the Strand. Presumably personal business of his, since otherwise he'd have met me at his office, but a solicitor nevertheless.

44

By the time I left the flat I'd given Nick enough to do to keep her busy. Some of it would be much easier if she talked — to other people, not to me — but I reckoned that she would, without me listening.

This appointment, I arrived first. The brasserie was empty — only just opened for the day — heavy dark wood panelling, brass fittings around the booths and at the bar, and two slim dark young French waiters looking sour and un-welcoming in a booth at the back.

I sat down near the front, ignored the waiters who were ignoring me, and amused myself by guessing what Adrian Trigg, solicitor, would look like. I'd worked for one of his partners three months back. The partner had looked like a well-presented pig with dolphin overtones.

Trigg arrived ten minutes late — the time it took for one of the waiters to slouch over to my table to take the order — and he wasn't a pig or a dolphin, he was a horse. In his early forties, tallish, in a formal dark suit with a long equine face, sandy hair and large protruding brown eyes with lots of whites showing round them, like a racehorse about to bolt. He was pan-icked, by me or by the situation. He poised his bum on the seat as if for quick escape and ordered, distractedly, a cup of chocolate, as if he hated chocolate but it was the only thing he could think of, and then took out a cigar-case and offered me one.

I refused. Then, belatedly, he said, 'You're Alex

Tanner, I suppose. I'm Adrian Trigg. Henry Plummer recommended you. He said you were discreet.'

'I am. Relax, Mr Trigg. I'm a tomb. Nothing you tell me will go any further.'

'Mind if I smoke?'

'Not at all.'

'I gave up cigarettes two years ago, but I'm still working on cigars. One a day, that's what I'm down to.'

'Well done.'

'Very important to take care of yourself. I keep fit. I play squash twice a week, and spend some time on the weights.'

'Right.'

He looked round, saw the waiters were out of earshot, and lit a cigar. His hands were shaking. 'It seems so disloyal,' he said.

'Are we talking about your wife?' I tried.

'It's because I trust her that I want to know,' he said. 'If I didn't trust her, then I wouldn't be surprised, d'you see what I mean?' And then, realizing that I'd mentioned his wife first, he looked at me suspiciously.

'A guess,' I said soothingly. 'Trust me.'

He crossed his legs, hitching up the cloth of his trousers so they didn't bag, revealing a pair of expensive black silk socks. His black shoes also looked expensive, and were shined to a high gloss. He wasn't an attractive man, at least not to me, but he was presentable, well-mannered, a partner in a top firm of solicitors: a classic meal-ticket for a moderately ambitious, conventional woman.

'Tell me about the problem.'

'It's Tuesday evenings. And the telephone call. And the shopping,' he blurted, and then paused while his chocolate and my coffee arrived.

I was making notes. 'The telephone call?'

'She was talking on the phone . . . I came in . . . she rang off.'

'Did you ask her who she was talking to?'

'Well, no . . . It would have looked as if . . .'

'As if you wanted to know,' I said. 'Which you did.'

'As if I didn't trust her.'

'Which you don't, completely, otherwise you wouldn't have hired me.'

'We've always been so — It's been perfect. Always. It's been perfect. I never knew what she saw in me, but from the first time we met — she said it was love at first sight, for her too. We just knew, both of us.'

It sounded more recent than I'd have guessed, for a man his age. 'When did you meet her?'

'Not quite six years ago.' He produced his wallet from his inside pocket and passed me a photograph. Blonde wife, twenty-something, pretty and slim in a swimsuit by a pool: three blond boys, four three two, in tiny swimsuits and happy smiles.

'Your pool?'

'Yes . . . We have a weekend place in Sussex. Isn't she perfectly beautiful?'

47

'Lovely. Your children?'

'Yes.'

'Charming children.'

'Yes,' he said, but with less emphasis. A wife man, not a son man.

'And apart from the telephone call, what else are you concerned about?'

'She goes out on Tuesday evenings. For about two hours.'

'Have you asked her where she goes?'

'Yes. She was . . . coy about it. She says women have secrets. But we have no secrets, none. This will probably sound very old-fashioned to you, and perhaps it is, but we have a traditional marriage. I earn the money, she looks after the home. She has no money of her own, you see, so I give her an allowance, and she always accounts to me for how she spends it. I don't ask her to, she says she wants to. That's how open we are with each other. Until now.'

The Triggs' traditional marriage didn't sound a bag of laughs, I thought, but I tried to reassure him. 'Only saying "women have secrets" doesn't sound very sinister. If she was meeting a lover, she'd lie. Make up a story for you.'

'Do you think so?' he said, pathetically encouraged.

'Probably,' I said. Unless she wants you to know, I added to myself. 'What does she wear?'

He looked at me blankly. 'How do you mean?'

'When she goes out on Tuesday evenings. Does

48

she dress up? Take special care with her appearance?'

'She always takes great care with her appearance,' he said repressively. 'She always looks absolutely perfect.'

I'd leave it, for the moment. 'And the shopping? You mentioned shopping.'

'Yes. Twice now, I've come into our bedroom when she was unpacking shopping bags, and I got the impression she was hiding something.'

'What kind of shopping bags?'

'How do you mean?'

'From Harrods? From Sainsbury's? From the off-licence?'

'Oh, I see . . . No, Arabella doesn't use plastic bags. The environment . . . She uses straw baskets. We brought them back from our honeymoon in Mexico.'

'What size were the packages?'

'She didn't let me see.'

I sipped at my coffee, which was excellent. I didn't want to take his case, which looked like the most predictable of sad domestics. It wouldn't take long to wrap up so I couldn't bill for much; he'd associate me with his humiliation and I could whistle for any more work from him.

'Mr Trigg, why don't you talk to her? Just ask her.'

'I can't. I can't . . . I'll pay you double your usual fee, Miss Tanner. I want a woman to do this. I don't want . . . to expose her, do you see? I just want to know. She's considerably youn-

49

ger than I am. She's very innocent. I wouldn't even be angry with her. I'd be hurt, of course, but — I just want to know.'

Chapter 5

So we did a deal. I'd find out where his wife went on Tuesday evenings, and let him know. He'd pay me a flat rate for the job, plus expenses: a good rate since I reckoned the whole thing plus report would be maybe a day's work.

It left me with a bad taste in my mouth on the tube home. Adrian Trigg came over as Mr Would-Be-Ideal Husband, a bit narrow, a bit of a romantic, very reliable; but I'd only talked to him for half an hour. Marriages are a mystery. I didn't want to be involved. But I was touting for hire and he'd hired me to do something which was harmless, on the face of it.

I decided not to think about it until I had to, on Tuesday night.

I got back to the flat at one-thirty to be greeted by the clatter of the word-processor keyboard. Peter must have gone out; a cleaner, smarter Nick was typing up the final notes on my latest piece of television work, screening interviews of Real People who'd applied to take part in a projected new game show. I'd been interviewing for two days in a hotel in Bournemouth, seen over seventy candidates, and managed to find eight possibles. The rest had been too Real for television.

She stopped when I came in, and turned to face me. She didn't smile but the muscles in her jaw twitched and I took a smile as read. 'Hi,' I said. 'Want some lunch?'

She nodded.

'Sandwiches do you?'

She nodded again.

'Come and listen to me while I make them.'

I set to work in the kitchen. She'd have to have cheese, and like it: I'd squirrelled away supplies from the Bournemouth hotel cheeseboard. It wasn't good but it was free.

She perched herself on a stool at the kitchen table and pushed a small box towards me. She'd managed my first assignment, anyway. Fifty cheap business cards: address and telephone number, plus

ALEX TANNER INVESTIGATIONS
Nick Straker, Assistant

I'd thought it would please her. It probably had. 'Do you have a handbag that isn't a plastic carrier?' I asked.

She shook her head.

'Do you mind a bum-bag?'

She shook her head.

My last assistant had left behind her Gucci bum-bag. It was sitting on the work-surface beside the knife-block. Claudia might want it back: she wouldn't get it. She could afford to buy twenty more. I pointed to it. 'It's yours. Use it for expenses money, business cards and your notebook.'

Nick picked up the bag, examined it, pointed to the Gucci clasp and sketched a question mark in the air.

'Yes, it's Gucci.'

She made a T with her fingers, then pointed to me.

'Thank you?'

She nodded.

'No sweat,' I said. 'It isn't mine and I don't wear bumbags . . . Coffee or tea?'

She sketched a C. I gave her black coffee, a carton of milk and the sugar, instead of asking her how she took it. The heartwarming non-verbal communication was starting to get up my nose. I put the sandwiches on the table, sat down and said 'Right. How much have you done?'

It was notebook time. *All of it,* she wrote.

'Including the autopsy on the hamster?'

They call it a post-mortem. It'll take maybe a day if you only want gross findings, longer if you want histology. I said gross findings to start with, it's cheaper. We're to ring back tomorrow.

She passed me the receipt, from a veterinary practice just off Notting Hill.

I was impressed. And I didn't know what histology was. Did she? 'What A Levels are you doing?'

Maths, Further Maths, Physics, Chemistry. I'm going to be a doctor.

'Any particular specialism?'

Anything but a psychiatrist, she wrote. *They're all wankers.*

She could tell me about it some other time. Listening to an adolescent on her life and times was dull enough; reading it would be insupportable. And we had work to do.

She listened impassively to my account of my dealings to date with the Womun in the Balaclava Helmet, looked at the letter that had come with the hamster, now safely inside a plastic wallet in case there were any fingerprints on it, and gave me her transcription of Jordan's telephone message, with the addresses and telephone numbers of Driscoll and Macarthy. Macarthy lived in West Hampstead (quite expensive, not far), I already knew Slater lived just off Kensington High Street (very expensive, quite near), and Driscoll in Herefordshire, about three hours' driving away. Her address gave me no clue to her affluence or occupation. Forge House, near Leadington, could be a tumbledown shack or a miniature mansion.

My main intention was to warn them, just in case there was malice behind the Womun's eccentricity. I'd only been paid for a day's work so I didn't expect to find out much, but I didn't want to be responsible for a disaster either. Just telling them what had happened might be enough. One or all of them might be able to identify the Womun and warn the others, even if they didn't want to tell me.

The obvious place to start was with Melanie Slater. She was closest and I knew her. And, most important of all, she was the first live person on the list. If it was a hit list, chances were she'd be next to be hit.

I rang her. She was in and she remembered me. She'd see me at four o'clock. She agreed reluctantly, and tried to get me to explain on the telephone. 'I'd rather not,' I said. 'I'm now working as a private detective and I have reason to believe that you're being threatened.'

'Threatened?' she said sharply. 'In what way?'

It sounded as if I'd hit a nerve. 'In any way. Have there been any incidents?'

'What kind of incident?'

'Anything at all threatening.'

'I've no idea what you're talking about,' she said dismissively, but she clearly did. Something had happened, but she wasn't going to tell me on the phone.

'I'd prefer to discuss it in person, just in case it's serious. You might be in a better position to judge that than I am.'

'I hope this isn't a joke,' she said doubtfully. I thought I understood her dilemma. She broadcast a lot, mostly on radio, sometimes on television, an instant pundit on Family Life, the Role of Women and the decay of Moral Values in the Younger Generation. The fees must have been sizeable, and the publicity helped her book sales. So she needed to keep in with the media and she had enough experience to know how influential researchers could be. She didn't want to offend me.

But she hadn't liked me, and she didn't want to waste time, and she had something to hide. So I nudged her a little. 'Don't bother, if you're too pressed. I've other contacts I can use.'

'Oh, come, by all means. Can you manage four o'clock at my house?'

I looked at my watch. No watch. Barty. Oh shit. I looked at the video clock: not yet three. 'Four o'clock would be fine.'

I presented myself at the smart stucco-fronted semi-detached house in the wide tree-lined street dead on time. I'd left Nick behind: I wasn't taking her on any interviews until she talked. She soon would.

It took Melanie a while to answer the bell. I stood on the doorstep, trying to remember the names of her children. I'd met them when I'd interviewed her — a prim little blonde goody-goody girl, sixish, and a lanky dark fifteen-year-old boy who'd been surprisingly good company. Bella and Teddy, that was it. Enquiries about them might break the ice.

Then she opened the door, unsmiling. She was wearing a shortish straight pale green skirt, a white silk blouse and a semi-fitted dark green linen jacket, shiny black tights (or they could have been stockings and suspenders as part of a Woman's duty to keep herself Attractive for her Man) and high-heeled black shoes. She had a narrow spindly little body, bony knees, and a slightly scrawny neck which could have done with more disguise than her heavy gold chain afforded. It was impossible to tell what colour her hair was naturally: it was as I remembered, dyed dark blonde with highlights, worn short and brushed upward in moussed, lacquered wings away from her carefully made-up face.

When I first met her I'd thought her smug. She didn't seem that today. A gracious hostess on the surface; defensive, perhaps even unhappy underneath. It might be significant, it might not. I expected to be taken to her study on the ground floor, or maybe even downstairs to the kitchen. When I'd been at the house before I'd never been taken upstairs. But she led me up the thickly carpeted stairs towards what she called the 'drawing-room' (though judging by her traces of regional accent I'd have bet her mother wouldn't have used the word — sitting-room, perhaps, or lounge). She sat me down on one of a pair of matching cream sofas that faced each other across a substantial coffee table in front of the fireplace, and perched herself on the other sofa, legs crossed at the ankle, hands folded in her lap, with the light behind her.

It was a conventionally furnished L-shaped room, decorated in shades of blue and cream. No bookshelves. Plenty of wall space; a display cabinet filled with china shepherds and shepherdesses; some silhouettes, miniatures, and

Victorian hunting prints. On the mantelpiece, invitations.

On a side table between the long windows, family photographs. Teddy from about six to adolescence; Bella from infancy to about eight; a wedding photograph with Julie as a bride in a cream silk suit, her husband (Nigel? Some name like that — I hadn't met him, but he'd been quoted a lot) in morning dress, and Teddy as a page, looking rebellious in silk knee-breeches and buckled shoes, evidence presumably of Melanie's mid-career conversion to the Sanctity of Marriage.

No sign at all of Teddy's father. I'd wanted to find out about him when I worked on her before but my producer, a pusillanimous idiot called Protheroe, told me not to waste time on irrelevancies. I didn't think it was irrelevant. If Melanie Slater had been a single mother, then surely her experience had a bearing on her views. If she'd been married and widowed, or if her husband had simply gone to the pub for a rest from GBH of the earhole and, wisely, never come back, why didn't she mention him?

Judging from the photographs, Melanie wanted to wipe out all her pre-Nigel past. Maybe Nigel was a jealous man who wanted no reminders. Maybe Melanie preferred to be born-again.

Contemporary Melanie, looking like an illustration from *Hello!* magazine, said, 'Can you get to the point, Alex? My daughter Bella will be home from school any minute now and I want to spend time with her. Tea and hot buttered

58

crumpets and chat. I really think it's important to be here for her when she comes in, so she feels loved, now the nights are closing in.'

'How are Bella and Teddy?' I said, hoping for less formality in her manner.

If anything, it congealed further. 'They are quite well,' she said. 'How can I help you?'

So I told her about the Womun in the Balaclava Helmet, and passed her a copy of the letter to look at. The sequence of events sounded sillier every time I recounted it.

Halfway through my account she relaxed, and when she read the letter she gave a knowing insider's smile. She didn't react to the hamster, and I found that odd. Perhaps she was expecting it. 'Do you know who the Womun in the Balaclava Helmet might be?' I said.

'Heavens, no,' she said, but not as if she cared if I believed her. 'Did you really expect me to be frightened of this crackpot?'

'I wanted to warn you,' I said mildly. 'And I thought you might know who it was.'

'You've warned me,' she said. 'I have no idea what prompted any of this nonsense, or who might be responsible. What I do know is that poor Leona died by accident.'

'The names on the list . . . I believe you were all members of a women's group, in Oxford. The Vestal Virgins. Is that right?'

'Yes. But that was a long time ago, and I have no idea what could have prompted this nonsense.'

'Are you all still friends? Do you keep in touch?'

'Poor Leona is dead.'

'Before she was dead, did you keep in touch? And what about the other two?'

'I've changed my views considerably since Oxford. That was a long time ago.'

'But are they still friends of yours, even if you don't agree with them politically?'

She sighed impatiently. 'Yes, they're friends, and we meet occasionally. But I have no idea what could have prompted this nonsense.'

She was stuck in a groove, and I couldn't shift her. That was her technique. Pick a form of words and stick to them. It made negotiation tedious and progress impossible, but she often emerged from a verbal wrangle on the media apparently victorious because anyone only half listening remembered what she'd said. It was like talking to a politician.

I'd found it irritating when I first met her. Now the old irritation came back in full flood. I kept going, though. I'd been paid. 'You can't think of anyone who might have a grudge against the Vestal Virgins?'

'No. It was a long time ago. Besides, it can't be serious. Poor Leona died by accident.'

I heard the front door open and close, admitting a set of footsteps, then a child's voice called, 'Mummy? Mummy?'

'Just coming, darling. Teddy? Are you there?'

'What d'you think?' came a sulky male mumble.

'Take Bella downstairs and put the kettle on. I have a visitor; she's just leaving.'

'Mummy? Mummy?' called Bella. 'Mummy, are we going to have Mopsy's funeral now? Mummy?'

'In a minute, darling. Go downstairs with Teddy,' said Melanie with a distinct edge to her tone.

I made for the door before she could uncross her ankles, went down the stairs two at a time and smiled as winsomely as I could manage at the little girl, a pervert's dream in her school uniform and white socks, who was swinging on the banisters. 'Hi, Bella. I'm Alex, remember? We met a while ago. Who's Mopsy?'

I was counting on one of Melanie's central Family Values being respect for your elders. She'd done a good job on Bella. 'Hello, Alex,' said the child politely. 'Mopsy's my hamster. She died yesterday.'

Chapter 6

It was a short-lived triumph which soon disintegrated into a scrum in the hall. Melanie's *Hello!* hostess image splintered completely. She came down the stairs at high speed — I'd have broken my neck if I'd tried that in her stilt-like heels — and opened the door. 'Goodbye,' she said firmly to me, and hissed 'Downstairs!' at Bella, whose mouth began to turn down in what I was sure would emerge as a wail. So, probably, was Melanie, because she softened it to 'Go downstairs for Mummy, please. Mummy wants to say goodbye to her visitor.'

'Poor Mopsy,' I said to Bella. 'What did she die of?'

'Over-feeding, I expect,' said a deep male voice, and Teddy appeared at the back of the hall, presumably from the stairs leading down to the kitchen.

'Teddy!' warbled Melanie, trying to sound affectionate and indulgent. 'Please take Bella downstairs and put the kettle on.'

'It's on,' said Teddy unhelpfully. He'd grown: he was over six feet now, and his jaw and Adam's apple were much more prominent. He was wearing shiny black school trousers which hung low on his hips, a once-white shirt half-untucked, and a frayed school tie: no longer smart-looking as he had been, not even tidy, with straggly un-washed hair. When he saw me, he obviously rec-ognized me. The sulky reluctance in his manner disappeared, to be replaced by puppyish self-conscious pleasure. He took a half-step towards me and flapped his hands by his sides as if he wanted to make a physical gesture but couldn't find an appropriate one.

'Hi, Teddy. I'm Alex Tanner. Remember me?' I said lightly.

'Of course,' he said, wriggled, and clasped his hands behind his back. 'You work in television. You were the researcher on that Family Values programme.'

I was pleased by his evident pleasure, then took a pull at myself and felt a fool. I must be desperate for attention if I wanted Teddy's.

'Mopsy just died,' said Bella poutingly. 'She didn't die of feeding. It was time for her to go to Hamster Heaven, Mummy said.'

'And where is Mopsy now?' I pressed on. I thought I knew the answer: under the scalpel of Evans and Wright Veterinary Surgeons.

'Mummy put her in the conservatory until we could have a proper funeral,' said Bella.

'Show me,' I said, taking Bella's hand. The child moved trustfully towards the back of the hall, and I followed.

'Really, Alex, I don't think —' began Melanie, but Teddy interrupted.

'Don't bother, Alex,' he said. 'The hamster's

63

gone. It had gone last night, after the break-in.'
Melanie glared at him. He smiled cheerfully,
pleased to have annoyed her, I thought.

'Goodbye, Alex,' said Melanie, and took my
arm. I let go of Bella's hand and let Melanie
urge me towards the front door.

' 'Bye,' said Teddy. 'See you around?'

I waved to him. He waved back, obviously relieved to find an acceptable and appropriate use
for at least one of his arms. It was a long arm,
with a large hand and a very bony wrist.

Still waving, I said to Melanie, 'The break-
in?'

'There is nothing more to discuss. You came
to warn me, and you've warned me. Poor Leona's
death was an accident. Now please leave.'

'Don't you think the hamster sent to me was
probably yours?'

'There is nothing more to discuss,' she said,
and closed the door in my face. The last thing
I saw was Teddy's basketball-player's hand
spidering his farewell.

Back in the kitchen of my flat, I watched Nick
make us coffee. I didn't think she'd ground beans
before — maybe she hadn't even made real coffee
— but she'd seen me do it earlier and she was
coping. A quick learner.

When she'd finished she sat down at the table
and began scribbling away.

*You think she knows who the Womun is. Maybe
it's her?*

64

'I don't think so. The Womun's voice didn't sound like hers, and, besides, she's not odd enough. She's very straightforward. I can't imagine her writing anonymous notes and packing up rodents in parcels.'

Why did she suddenly decide to get rid of you when the children came back?

'Probably she didn't want me to know it was Bella's hamster. Maybe she didn't want the child upset about her pet. Or perhaps she didn't want me to hear about the break-in. I'm sure the break-in was what she was worried about when we talked on the phone. She stopped worrying when I told her about the Womun.'

How involved do you think she is?

'Practically, not at all, I'm sure. And I'm beginning to lose interest, because she doesn't think it's a real threat and she obviously knows far more about the Womun than I do. She wants the whole thing covered up, but not out of fear for her own safety.'

So what are we going to do next? wrote Nick.

'*We* are not going to do anything unless you stop this bloody silly non-speaking lark. It's going to slow me down, and I won't have it. It's decision time, Nick. You can come back tomorrow on two conditions. One, that you go back to sleep at your foster parents' place tonight. I don't want you on the street, it's dirty.' It was also dangerous, but I wouldn't say that.

I thought maybe I could sleep here? she wrote.

'Absolutely no way.'

What's the second condition? she wrote.

'That, tomorrow, you talk.'

'I'll talk today,' she said. 'No problem. I'm quite normal. There's nothing wrong with me.'

I wasn't surprised, but I pretended to be: I'd allow the kid her small victories. 'Hey!' I said. 'You've got a voice.' It was a good voice, too; deep and rich. It sounded like a night-club singer's from the forties, with a crack in it. The accent was London, but not broad London: there were consonants among the vowels.

'Of course I have,' she said. 'I don't talk to wankers, that's all. But I'm not going back to the Barratts' place. I hate it. I hate them.'

We stared at each other. 'OK,' I said finally. 'Come to work at eight tomorrow, that'll give you enough time for a bath.'

'What are we going to do tomorrow?'

'I'll tell you then.'

I wasn't being secretive: I didn't know myself. I closed the door behind her with relief, went back into the kitchen, turned on Classic FM, listened to three or four bars of a soprano belting out popular opera (Mozart? Puccini?) and switched her off again, mid-screech. I hate sopranos, solo violins and midnight cats.

I should ring Barty, but not yet. I scribbled some notes to myself and stuck them up on my 'work in progress' cork-board, beside Jordan's article, the photographs of the Vestal Virgins and the Womun's list.

Melanie Slater's break-in?
Leona Power: accident?
Ring Macarthy and Driscoll

I looked at the board. After Melanie's reaction, nothing seemed so urgent, now.

When Peter came back, ten minutes later, he brought the wood for my spare-room bookshelves, bought from a friend at a cut rate. He never bought anything from a normal shop, if he could help it. He always knew a man who knew a man who had top quality whatever it was cheap, know what I mean? I didn't know precisely what he meant and I didn't ask, though I assumed it had walked from a film set or a building site.

It was top quality hardwood. It didn't have any distinguishing marks. I still didn't like it. I'll take cheese from a hotel cheeseboard, I'll pad my expenses, but I don't steal. It's one of the lines I draw for myself. And I didn't much want to receive stolen goods.

On the other hand, Peter wouldn't have understood. He thought he was doing me a favour; and I don't like offending friends, either. I don't have that many real friends.

So I thanked him and admired the wood and got out my Black and Decker Workmate from the cupboard under the stairs and showed him where the tools were kept, and went out to buy the ingredients for the spaghetti supper he said he wanted, and plenty of wine.

Tuesday, 28 September

Chapter 7

The alarm went off at seven-thirty and I woke feeling happy without knowing why. I lay in bed sipping mineral water from the bottle I'd left on the bedside table (clue: I must have been half-smashed and brought the water up to ward off dehydration), looking at the ceiling, and clawing my way back to consciousness. Ceiling. Barty. I waited for the rush of embarrassment: it came, but half-strength. I didn't blush.

Then I remembered. The night before, somewhere during the second bottle of wine, I'd decided what to do about seeing him. It had seemed exhilaratingly right at the time. It still looked right now. It had two great assets: simplicity and honesty.

I'd take my morning run up to his house (which would save me from having to dress up for him), pick up my watch, cadge breakfast, and tell him I was sorry it had all gone wrong and I didn't know what to do. Then see how it went. I was almost looking forward to it.

I went down to the kitchen for coffee and was pleasantly surprised by the lack of clutter. I'd wimped out at eleven the night before and left Peter to clear up. The cooker was splashed with tomato sauce, the saucepans were still soaking and he'd wiped the work surfaces with a tea-towel, but apart from that he hadn't done a bad job.

Two cups of coffee and a glass of water later I was alive enough to wash and dress. I stuck my head out of the bathroom window to get a fix on the weather: overcast, maybe rain later, but quite warm — over sixty degrees already. I put on my brightest-coloured T-shirt, light blue, my newest pair of tracksuit bottoms, and an extra dollop of moisturizer. My hair's very short so there were no major decisions to be made there, but I moussed it and rubbed my fingers through the roots a few times for lift.

I don't look at my face very much, but doing my hair I couldn't avoid it. I have green eyes. They looked especially green: they do, when I'm happy. So I changed to a green T-shirt for consistency, put on my Reeboks and went down to my desk in the living-room to write a note to stick on the door for Nick, warning her to keep ringing the bell till she woke Peter.

On my desk, next to the telephone, was my watch.

I expected it so little that at first I didn't see it, but pushed it aside to take some paper. Then I registered.

'Peter! Peter!' I shouted in a work voice. 'In here. Now!'

He stumbled from the spare room wearing only his natural pelt of hair (I'd forgotten quite how hairy he was) and a pair of boxer shorts with

'Goodnight' printed all over them in different languages. 'What is it?'

'How did my watch get here?'

'Is that all?' he groaned. 'Do you have any orange juice?'

'Not till you answer my question.'

He collapsed on to the sofa. 'Barty O'Neill came by last night. After you'd crashed out. After I'd crashed out, come to that. I let him in and told him you were in bed, and he left the watch and went. I'd've given him a drink but he seemed pissed off. Funny, that. He's an easy-going bloke usually.'

'What were you wearing?'

'This.'

'Just the boxer shorts?'

'Yes.'

I went to get him the orange juice, to give myself time to think. Barty must have leapt to the wrong conclusion, like someone in a cheap romantic novel. He must have thought I was sleeping with Peter. I understood the misunderstandings in a romance: the author had to stretch out the plot. It was bloody annoying if it had happened in real life, and maybe I was flattering myself that he'd mind. But Peter was right. Barty'd worked with Peter but he didn't know him well, and Barty's manners are on the smooth side of good; under normal circumstances even if he'd felt pissed off he wouldn't have let Peter see it.

I could just pick up the telephone and sort it

out there and then, but I didn't want to be over-heard. I'd have to get Peter out of the flat first.

I went back into the living-room. 'Here's your juice.'

'Thanks. Hey, I just thought of something. You told me last year Barty fancied you. Maybe he's jealous.'

'Maybe he is,' I said snappishly.

'Then I've done you a favour, haven't I? You said last year you didn't fancy him. So if he thinks you're spoken for, he'll lay off, won't he, no bones broken.'

'That was last year,' I said. There must have been something in my tone, because Peter stopped kidding and sat up.

'Shit, Alex, don't tell me he's the love of your life.'

'There ain't no such thing.'

'Flavour of the month?'

'Flavour of the week, anyway.'

I sat down on the sofa beside him and he put an arm around me. 'What's the state of play with you two, then? Has he had his leg over?'

'No,' I said. I shrugged off his arm but I didn't get up. I wanted his comments. He was about as different from Barty as a man could be, but that still left him with insights I couldn't have, because he was male and I wasn't.

'Has he tried?'

'Yes. And then I tried to let him. The night before last. While you were watching the rugby, when my parcel arrived.'

74

'You *tried* to let him? Couldn't he get it up? Poor guy.' He gave a smug, MCP chuckle and I stamped on his bare foot with my Reebok. Not very hard.

He howled anyway. 'What's that for? I'm being caring, for Chrissake, and before breakfast.'

'It was me, Peter. My fault. I was frightened.'

'*Frightened?* Of sex? You?'

He was genuinely astonished, and I was surprised.

'I didn't want to be a disappointment to him.'

'In bed? That doesn't make sense. You're fine in bed. It's out of it you can be such a bossy ball-busting cow, but he must know that anyway.'

It was my turn to be astonished. 'I'm fine in bed?'

'Better than fine. A natural. But let me get this straight. The night before last he takes you to bed and it goes down like a concrete overcoat. Last night he drops by to have another go, and gets me in my boxers? No wonder the poor guy was pissed off. He'd be sensitive, too, at his age.'

'He's not old.'

'Well over forty.'

'Forty-three.'

'OK, whatever. You've got to explain, Alex. Give him a bell now.'

'I will as soon as you're dressed and out.'

'Do I have to? Can't I just get in the bath, run the water and sing "Bat out of Hell"? I couldn't listen then.'

'I'd know you were there. And I hate Meatloaf.

75

And the caff on the corner does great bacon sarnies.'

He went, grumbling, to dress and I went for more coffee.

Then Nick arrived, plastic bags and all. She nodded at me as I let her in.

I wasn't in the mood for games. 'Good morning,' I said. 'Answer me in words, or you're fired.'

'Good morning,' she mumbled. I pointed in the direction of the stairs and she headed on up. I didn't mind her being in the flat while I talked; she didn't count.

'Ten minutes,' said Peter on his way through. 'Then I'm back, so get your lovers' quarrel sorted sharpish.'

I shut the flat door behind him and listened for his footsteps down the stairs and Nick's bathwater running before dialling Barty.

Three rings, then a pick-up. I was prepared for Barty or for the answerphone but it was neither. It was a woman's voice, the sort of perky customer-relations-trained voice that tries to sell you double-glazing.

'Mr O'Neill's answering service. Can I help you?'

Answering service? What was this?

'Can I speak to Mr O'Neill, please?'

'I'm afraid he's not currently available. May I take a message?'

I wasn't about to tell her that Alex Tanner wasn't bonking Peter Barstow, which was the only message I had. 'Is Barty away?'

'I'm afraid I'm not permitted to divulge that information,' said the voice.

Stuff it, I thought. 'Just say Alex Tanner rang,' I managed, and rang off.

The rest of the morning was work. I rang Grace Macarthy's number. I didn't have particularly high hopes: she was genuinely famous, very likely to be away or busy or too important to see me, but she lived closeish so I tried her first. She was in. She answered the phone; she bubbled over at me. She thought it sounded like fun, and was ready to see me any time that day.

Soon, was my answer. Work would take my mind off Barty. Work would keep Nick off my back and stop me having to talk to her. I very much wanted to be alone, but if I couldn't be, then better that Nick was concentrating on work rather than me.

When Nick came down fresh from her bath she looked like a normal teenager. She'd put on a baseball cap; it covered all her bare patches of scalp. Now I could see what the unharmed fringe round her lower scalp was for. Her hair-cutting was a crafty and premeditated piece of self-mutilation because it left her to a certain extent presentable. If the person you were presenting her to didn't mind baseball caps.

Grace Macarthy apparently didn't. She answered her own door very soon after I rang the bell of her ramshackle terraced West Hampstead house. 'Alex Tanner? And . . . ?'

I introduced Nick. Grace gave us both a wide smile and a friendly, determined handshake. She looked as if she'd been working out, sweating a little, wearing leotard, tights, legwarmers, and a sweatband round her forehead. She had a strong, young-looking body and the well-known hawklike face, with mid-brown permed hair piled on top of her head, and knowing eyes. The face was more lined than I'd expected.

'Thanks for seeing us at such short notice,' I said as we followed her through a dark narrow hall cluttered with two bicycles, several black plastic rubbish bags and a rowing machine, towards an amateurish-sounding version of one of the songs from *Cabaret* played on keyboard and drums.

The hall smelt of dry rot. I'd smelt it several times in the six months I'd flat-hunted, a while back, and I hastily revised her house price downwards. I'd reckoned two hundred thousand: it was a tall, narrow Victorian terraced house on four floors and a basement, probably five bedrooms, two bathrooms, in a shabby but rising residential area. But if the house had dry rot God only knew what the repairs could cost, and I'd noticed settlement cracks around the front doorway.

She stopped and turned to me when I spoke and said, 'The workmen start on the dry rot next week.'

She'd guessed what I was thinking. Her eyes were not just knowing but quick, I realized, and

I cranked up my reactions a notch. She wouldn't be easy to read. 'Really?' I said. 'Poor you.'

'I like workmen,' she said, and gave a sexy chuckle. 'Talking of which' — she led us into a long room which took up the entire ground floor apart from the hall — 'meet Tadeuscz and Frederic; Alex and Nick.'

They were in their late twenties, probably Poles, judging from the names. Certainly Eastern Europeans from their flashy cheap clothes and pale pasty faces. The one at the keyboard was tall, broad and tasty, with long blond locky hair. The one on drums was shorter, narrower and darker.

They both stood up and bowed. 'Tadeuscz,' said the dark one.

'Frederic,' said the blond one. Standing up, he was really tall — almost as tall as Barty, who's six-four.

Nick nodded. 'Hi,' I said.

'Help yourself to coffee if you'd like some and grab yourselves chairs,' said Grace, 'then hang on for ten minutes or so, if you don't mind. We need to finish rehearsal before Tad and Fred go to work.'

'What are you rehearsing for?' I said, waving Nick towards the instant coffee and kettle visible near the large Aga range.

'We're doing a turn for Children in Need,' said Grace. She was being considerate, or patronizing, saying 'we', because there was no way the great British public would want to see Tad and Fred making fools of themselves. It was Amazin' Grace

79

Macarthy they'd want to see.

I sat listening to Tad and Fred stumble through the intro to the song, and then Grace started to sing. She didn't exactly sing. She said the words, on the beat, with much interpretation. It wasn't a musical rendering but it was powerful and rather dramatic. Not at all like Liza Minelli. Nor was her voice quality particularly like the Womun's voice on my tape: too hard, too clear; though if she was even a passable mimic she could have adapted it.

Nick was very taken with her. She watched the song, and the dance, with close attention, while the kettle boiled, switched itself off and cooled down. I wasn't going to nag her. I rather enjoyed sitting alone in my own silence amid the noise, looking round the room.

It was one of the most jumbled rooms I've ever been in. It must have been forty feet long by about twenty wide. The end nearest the back of the house, where we were, was basically a kitchen, with the Aga range and the sink and fridge and work surfaces down each side and a long narrow scrubbed kitchen table in the middle, with wooden chairs round it, where I was sitting. The keyboard and drum kit were in a bay at the back, just in front of the windows leading to the garden beyond. The garden was a slope upwards: the house, like so many in that part of West Hampstead, was built on the side of a hill and probably had a deep damp cellar at the front.

The part of the room towards the front of the

80

house was a living-room. The walls were painted dark red. It had sofas and chairs, all in various stages of decline and dilapidation, and wall-to-ceiling bookcases except around the doors and the fireplace, which had last night's fire still smouldering. There were tables and chests against the walls and an eclectic accumulation of statues and boxes from any and every ethnic source. Some of them looked valuable. All of them were covered with a layer of fine ash from the wood fire, and several of the bowls held incongruous objects, like discarded coffee cups and a wellington boot.

The kitchen area was no less jumbled. Every work surface was entirely covered with objects, some predictable like a Moulinex mixer and several jars crammed with wooden spoons and spatulas, some of them less obviously kitchen, like a bulging expandable paper file, expanded to the limit of its powers and beyond, spilling bills and receipts and scraps of paper into the fruit bowl next to it, which was already piled high with oranges and blackening bananas and several tubes of hand cream.

How could she live like that? And how could one person generate so much clutter?

At last, Tad and Fred went to work. They were building labourers, apparently, and they wisely weren't giving up the day job. I was relieved when the front door closed behind them. Now, perhaps, we could get on with the interview. Besides, I was a touch irritated by the atmosphere of adulation. Tad, Fred and Nick all looked at Grace as if she was an unexploded bomb or the promise of all their futures.

I couldn't see it, myself, but then I'm not a groupie by temperament, and if I see everybody succumbing to someone's charm my instinct is to dig in my heels and refuse to budge. But, to be fair, she wasn't dull. In fact she was mildly exhilarating.

Not exhilarating enough to distract me, however. So with the departure of Tad and Fred I hoped we could get to the point, but Grace offered us toast and marmalade, as if she was taking care of us, and Nick picked up on that. Funny. Sudden melting of glacier. I'd thought she didn't like being taken care of, in fact with me she'd resisted it, but obviously Grace was different.

So we lived through the making of the toast in a toaster disinterred from a basket of laundry, and the adjustment of the shade of toast Nick wanted and the particular flavour of marmalade Nick wanted. Grace then played 'hunt the jar' and finally found the lemon marmalade in her drinks cupboard in the living-room area.

We'd been there over half an hour, by then, and I was beginning to lose patience. The room annoyed me. I feel clutter like a threat. The world is chaotic enough without letting the chaos into your house to lap around your knees, or in Grace's case around your throat.

When Nick was established with her toast, I started to talk to Grace, but she said: 'Hang on a minute. I think we should go to my study to talk, it'll be easier.'

Reluctantly, I followed her up the stairs. Nick would have followed her into heavy artillery fire. Grace opened a door on the first floor and led us into her study.

It was the neatest place I had ever seen. Filing cabinets, white walls, windows with blinds, a desk clear of everything except a small computer and a fax. Utterly different from everything else I had seen in the house.

She smiled at me. It was on the surface a warm, understanding smile, but I thought it mischievous. 'Alex will be happier here,' she said. 'Won't you, Alex?'

In one sense I was. In another, fundamentally, I wasn't. She was one of those people who specialize in instant character-readings, and on the evidence so far she was spot on. A clever woman.

People who think they're clever are often just a little less clever than they think they are, but Grace was turning out so unpredictable I wouldn't even rely on that, in her case. One thing I *was* absolutely sure of, and that was that I'd have to concentrate if I was going to get anything out of her, certainly if I was going to get anything that she didn't want to let me see. Good people-readers are also very good at deception because they know what clues not to give.

Before we even sat down I said, 'I expect Melanie Slater's told you most of the background.' I didn't know, of course, that Melanie had rung her, but the chances were that she had, and I didn't think that Grace would necessarily choose to lie.

She hesitated briefly before she answered, and I thought I was doing OK. 'She told me a little about it, yes. But I'd prefer to hear the story from you.' She sat down behind the bare desk, full of confidence, with the glow of fame about her like a halo.

I don't mind famous people; I meet a lot of them, and I'm not envious of their position. I'd hate not to be able to hide myself in a crowd. But I've often tried to work out where the glow comes from. Maybe they have it to start with, and that's why they succeed. Maybe it comes from being photographed so much that they glide automatically from pose to pose.

'Alex?' said Grace rather sharply into the pause. It hadn't hurt her to wait.

'I was wondering why famous people glow,' I said.

She laughed. Heartily, as if what I'd said was funny. Which it wasn't.

Nick laughed too, loyal to Grace.

I sat in silence, waiting.

Eventually Grace spoke. 'Why don't you like me, Alex?'

I'd waited her out. A small victory. Which, judging by the amusement in her eyes, she didn't see as a victory at all.

'Does it matter?' I said. 'Nick, tell Grace the story, please.'

Chapter 8

'Wasn't she amazing?' said Nick in the car on our way home. Not my car: I can't afford one. My friend Polly's new black Golf GTi, which she's letting me use while she's in Hong Kong.

'I suppose that's where she got her name.'

'What name?'

'Her nickname: Amazin' Grace.'

'Like the song? I didn't know she was called that . . . It makes all kinds of sense, though. Yeah, it fits.' She stared dreamily ahead. 'When you went to the toilet, she said I could stay at her place, if I wanted.'

'And do you want?'

'I don't know . . . Yeah, I do, but I might get on her nerves, and I couldn't stand that, to watch her eyes cloud over. I bet they do; what do you think, Alex?'

'About her eyes? Nothing at all.' About Nick, I was thinking plenty. Mary'd asked me to look after her, and I wasn't sure throwing her to Grace Macarthy would come under that heading. 'Nick, are you gay?'

'Sure,' said Nick. 'Are you?'

'No,' I said. 'Not even bi. What d'you think about Grace? Is she?'

'Hope so,' said Nick. 'I'm not sure. She might

85

just be a great human being.'

Or she might want to get her hooks in a vulnerable kid as fuel for the roaring furnace of her ego. On the other hand, she might want to keep an eye on my investigation.

If so, she'd hidden her interest well. She'd listened to Nick's account of my client's odd behaviour, read the letter, and seemed helpful and open. She had no idea who it might be. She had no idea what the letter might mean. She was sure Leona's death had been an accident. She was very grateful for my warning.

She'd been so blandly, obstructively noncommittal that I'd gone to the toilet to leave them alone together to see if she'd pump Nick. 'When I was in the toilet, what did you talk about?'

'Me. She asked about me. She said she could see I was an unusual person. I told her all about myself. She was interested. People always ask me, but they're only pretending to listen, waiting for me to stop talking so they can tell me what they'd decided to tell me anyway.'

'She didn't talk about the case?'

'What case?'

'The investigation. The letter, the parcel, the Womun.'

'Oh, that. No. Nothing.' Nick did some more dreamy staring, then said, 'Alex, she's the most exciting thing that's happened to me. Ever.'

I was supposed to be giving her work experience, not acting as a dating agency. Some time soon I'd have to start giving her pointers, about loyalty to your boss and about concentration on the task at hand. Not yet, though. I'd let her take her dream and run with it, for a while.

Back at the flat, there were no answerphone messages. I sent Nick to the kitchen to make scrambled eggs for lunch so I didn't have to watch her yearning about, and got on the phone.

I tried Elspeth Driscoll's number first. A high-pitched whine. Checked with the operator: line out of order. I reported the fault, then dialled West End Central police station looking for Eddy Barstow, Peter's father. After five minutes of re-routing I got him.

He sounded jovial and pleased with himself. 'So what can I do you for, Alex? Tell your Uncle Eddy.'

I explained what I wanted, while he made notes: details of Melanie Slater's break-in, if she'd reported it, and the lowdown on Leona Power's accident, if there was any. He whistled. 'When do you want it?'

'ASAP. Tomorrow morning would do.'

'Breakfast time? D'you want me to call you or nudge you?'

'Call me, Eddy. This info's not worth the ultimate sacrifice.'

'Bollocks, gal. You'd enjoy it, trust me. I'd show you a good time, and young Peter tells me you've lost your nerve in the bedroom area, so I'd be doing you a favour.'

'When did he tell you that?'

'He gave me a bell this morning.'

I was narked. I've never believed that women were bigger gossips than men, but this beat the jungle-drum speed record. 'He should keep his mouth shut,' I said.

'Don't be like that. We're family, with your best interests at heart. Young Peter's very fond of you.'

'He called me a bossy ball-busting cow.'

'That's what I just said, he's fond of you.'

His sweaty good nature was getting on my teeth, but I wanted the info, so I kidded along for another minute before I rang off, making a mental note to give Peter a hard time later.

'Food's ready when you want it,' said Nick.

After lunch I needed a break from Nick. I changed into my running gear again — no green T-shirt for me this time, my eyes were back to disappointed hazel — left Nick to decide where she was spending the night and fix up the details with Grace Macarthy if she needed to, and to ring the vet's for any results on the hamster, and headed up Ladbroke Grove towards Notting Hill and Barty.

He'd hired the answering service to annoy me, I knew it. Nobody in the media used services any more. The mobile or the answerphone covered it if you didn't have an assistant, which at the moment he actually did. So he was deliberately keeping away from me. Maybe he was angry. I'd seen him angry with other people, and it wasn't a pretty sight.

If he was at home, I'd speak to him. If he wasn't, I'd grill his assistant, if she was there.

There was no sign of life in the house, nor in his office in the basement. I rang both bells until the futility was too obvious for further pretence. Then I ran round Holland Park for twenty minutes, then I ran home, sprinted up the stairs, and collapsed on the sofa. I was knackered. And furious.

Nick was radiant with excitement. 'Don't tell me,' I said. 'You've signed on for an amazing night with Amazin' Grace.'

'I'm staying there all right, but Alex — listen, Alex — about the hamster.'

'What?' I said grumpily.

'It was murdered.'

The anger went first. I was still knackered, but now I was interested. 'How?' I said.

'Stabbed to the heart. With something very narrow and sharp, like an upholstery needle.'

'Why didn't I see the blood?'

'The vet says it wouldn't have bled much, externally, because the puncture was so narrow. And maybe it was cleaned up afterwards. How closely did you look?'

'Not very . . . I don't like dead things.'

'You'd never make a doctor, then.'

'And you'd never survive a week as an investigator, if you sleep with all the suspects,' I said snappily.

Nick was too excited to notice. 'Do you still

think it's Melanie Slater's hamster? And if so, why was it killed?'

'No idea,' I said. I hadn't. But I was now — and for the first time — really worried.

Chapter 9

Elspeth Driscoll's phone was still out of order when I tried it for the fourth time, at seven o'clock that evening. I stopped my mind churning out visions of her lying, stabbed to the heart by an upholstery needle, near a wrecked telephone in Forge House, deepest Herefordshire. My instinct was to drive straight down to her place, but I couldn't: I couldn't possibly manage the drive in under six hours, there and back, and at seven-thirty I had to be in shallowest Kensington, ready to follow Arabella Trigg to her love-tryst. If it was a love-tryst.

Once I'd done the business for Adrian Trigg then maybe I'd go to warn Elspeth Driscoll. Or discover her body.

At seven-twenty I was sitting alone (Nick had gone to yearn at Grace Macarthy) in a parked taxi about fifty yards up from Adrian Trigg's house and, coincidentally, only about two hundred yards from Melanie Slater's. Investigator to the Kensington set, that was me.

Two weeks ago I'd shared a takeaway pizza and video evening with my old mate Michelle and her two kids in her ninth-floor flat on the Fulham council estate where I'd grown up. Evenings with Michelle had to feature takeaways:

she's been agoraphobic ever since the estate gang raped her fifteen years back. The downside of the agoraphobia is that her choice of boyfriends is limited; the upside is that it's no skin off her nose that the lifts never work. She'd been on at me for my lack of social conscience, though she didn't put it that way. 'Why do you never work for our lot?' she'd said. 'Plenty of wrongs to right on the estate. Starting with the sodding loan-sharks.'

I'd given her some blag. But the truth was, if you lived on the estate, you couldn't afford me. Not on Social Security. And I had to live, didn't I?

And now the expensive door to the Triggs' expensive house was opening, and out came Arabella, just as pretty as her photograph. She got into a middle-range Mercedes and I said to my taxi-driver, 'That's her. And that's the car I want you to follow.'

I'd been lucky with my driver. He was a late middle-aged, world-weary Cockney who had no views on the political situation in Britain. None that he wanted to communicate, anyhow. So for once in a taxi I had a bit of peace.

He grunted, started the taxi and followed the Mercedes into Kensington High Street, all the way along to Hyde Park Corner, and north by the Park. We nearly lost her at Marble Arch but picked her up again travelling east in the one-way system just north of Oxford Street and followed her all the way to Harley Street, where she parked in one of the whopping great meter spaces provided by a thoughtful council for the top doctors' big cars.

My taxi pulled in to a parking space behind her. 'What d'you want me to do?' said my driver.

'Hang on for me a moment.' I hopped out of the taxi and followed Arabella along the road. She stopped at a lighted doorway, rang a bell and was almost immediately let in, before I reached her. I'd no idea which of the bells she'd rung but I waited until the door closed firmly behind her then nipped up the steps and wrote down the names on the brass plates by the door. Some were doctors and surgeons; some were just names, with letters after them that I didn't recognize. But I copied them all down and went back to the taxi.

'Ladbroke Crescent, please,' I said. I wasn't going to hang around until she came out: I'd enough information to be going on with. Either she was consulting one of these medical gentlemen or she was bonking him; I'd establish that tomorrow.

Eight-thirty, back at the flat, there was a note from Peter. *Out for the night. On to a good, blonde thing. See you at breakfast. Don't worry, you're an ace legover.*

Annoyed rather than encouraged by this cack-handed loyalty, I checked the answering machine — no messages — and tried Elspeth Driscoll again. The receiver whined at me. Still out of order.

I opened my french windows to my pseudo-balcony. The temperature had dropped to the mid-forties and there was a breeze blowing. I could do with a breeze. My head felt cluttered.

What to do now? If you padded the hours a tadge, which I usually did, I'd already worked nearly the day the Womun had paid me for. It didn't make sense to spend another six hours' worth — at least — on a wild-goose chase to the country, paying for my own petrol. Elspeth Driscoll might be away. She'd almost certainly, if she was there, be soundly asleep in her respectable bed. She might refuse to answer the door, after midnight. Her husband, if she had one, might be a country gentleman type with a shotgun who'd pepper me with pellets and prejudices.

But if I didn't go, and something happened to her, I'd regret it. I like to keep low deposits on my guilt-account.

Plus if I didn't go I'd certainly go round to Barty's again, which would be a terrible move. And I like driving alone, at night, in a free car, with Mahler playing on a high-quality stereo.

I found the village of Leadington easily enough, at a quarter past midnight. The last twenty minutes of the drive were through orchards and fields on the west side of the Malvern Hills, which gloomed over the dark landscape like the smooth humps of a mythical monster. The village itself was hicksville-on-ooze, a village shop and post

94

office, a pub, and several cottages clustered round the road and a smallish river. There were very few lights, and none of them were downstairs.

I parked by the pub and got out of the car.

It was almost cold, here, and almost silent, except for the sound of the river, and the air was fresh. Fresher than it ever was in London.

I think the country's overrated, but be fair, it's a rest-cure for your lungs. I put on my leather biker's jacket and walked up the main street resting my lungs and looking at the names on the cottages. None of them was Forge House, but I hadn't expected them to be. There were some flower-names (Rose, Honeysuckle and Violet); Hill Bank Cottage (no hill or bank in sight); Riverside Cottage (furthest from the river) and — promisingly — Nelson Mandela Cottage, with a light on upstairs.

I'd give that a whirl. They'd probably be least threatened by a late caller in a biker's jacket and DMs. I knocked on the front door (no bell), admired the push-chair and unidentifiable car parts rusting in the tiny weed-filled front garden, and waited.

Voices. Thump, thump down the stairs, and the door was opened by a man in his forties in a Greenpeace T-shirt and the kind of leather bikini briefs sold by specialist mail-order firms. More a thong, really.

I tried to talk to his face, not his thong, but it was a struggle. When he understood what I was after, he said, 'Oh sure. You want Elspeth.

95

Straight along here for a quarter of a mile, when the road forks take the left fork, it's just there on the right. You'll hear the barking.' Then he laughed, and added, 'Not just of the dogs.'

His voice was posh, like Barty's. His thong moved as he spoke. I thanked the thong and he closed the door.

I took the left fork, slowed down approaching some gates, and opened the electric windows. Sure enough, dogs. Plenty of them. I turned between the gates into a short, potholed, overgrown drive and stopped in front of a darkened house surrounded by trees.

The house looked dilapidated in the headlights: decaying windows, peeling paint on the front door, bricks overdue for pointing. It needed upkeep. But it was beautiful: Elizabethan, probably, without any obvious additions. Say six or eight bedrooms. If it had any land, apart from the front garden which was taken up by a large wooden structure, presumably kennels, it would be very valuable.

As I got out of the car a light went on upstairs, on the right. Then the hall light went on, and finally the door opened. A woman stood there, back-lit so I couldn't make out her features, with shortish fuzzy hair, skinny legs under a flannel nightshirt and a barrel body.

'Elspeth Driscoll?' I said.

'Ya,' she said cheerfully. 'Who wants her?'

'I'm Alex Tanner, a private investigator. Sorry

to disturb you at this time of night, but I was worried about you and your phone's out of order. I've reason to believe you're in danger. I've received threats.' I was almost shouting, to be heard over the barks.

'Threats? Who from?'

'I don't really know . . . A client who calls herself the Womun in the Balaclava Helmet.'

'*Belt up, darlings!*' she bellowed. The barking, briefly, stopped. When it did, all I could hear was Elspeth. She was giggling, irrepressibly, like an adolescent. 'You'd better come in and tell me about it,' she said between gasps. 'The Womun in the Balaclava Helmet, eh? I thought we'd buried her long since.'

Wednesday, 29 September

Chapter 10

'It was a joke, really,' she said. 'Twenty years ago. More. When we were all at Oxford. We had a feminist group, called —'

'The Vestal Virgins,' I said.

She was pleased. 'So you've heard of us! Brilliant! How much sugar in your cocoa?'

'Lots,' I said. We were in her kitchen. Large, stone-flagged, authentic country, draughty and cold. No fitted cupboards; an Aga, some tall cupboards with shelf tops displaying crockery, a whacking great wooden kitchen table scrubbed white, a sink from the forties and a fridge from the fifties.

'Bring your chair closer to the Aga,' she instructed, seeing me shiver. She'd put on a Barbour over her blocky middle-aged body and stuffed her bare feet into fleece-lined boots. She had a round, weatherbeaten, broken-veined face, brown eyes bright between puffy lids and bags, and greying dark hair which had been dyed and permed too long ago. I tried, but I couldn't place her at all as the girl in the photograph. She looked much older than Macarthy or Slater, but she sounded much younger. Her voice was light, bubbly and clear. It sounded middle-class, slightly dated, and innocent.

'We were an activist group,' she went on, handing me a mug and pulling a chair up beside me. 'We did things. But so we didn't get into trouble all the time we wore Balaclava helmets. So when I painted "Male Chauvinist Pig" on the door of the Master's Lodgings at Trinity, I wore a Balaclava helmet. In case I was seen. And that was how we signed ourselves.'

'So the Womun in the Balaclava Helmet could be any of you?'

She nodded cheerfully and giggled. 'It was any of us. Whoever was taking action, you see?'

'You or Grace or Leona or Melanie?'

'Yes, of course. Any of us. Like . . . the Saint with his drawing in the Leslie Charteris books. It was our signature. But that was yonks ago, as I said. What's the Womun done now?'

I told her the story and showed her the letter. I didn't tell her that the hamster had been stabbed. I intended to keep that information to myself until I'd made some sense of it.

When I'd finished, she said, 'I don't understand. You got a parcel with a *hamster* in it?'

'Yes.'

'A dead hamster?'

'Luckily for the hamster.'

'But that's ghastly. That's — sick.' She looked slightly sick herself. With all those dogs, perhaps she was an animal freak. Bomb humans so animals don't suffer, that kind of thing.

'Do you know what all this is about?' I said. 'Do you know who's doing it, and what they mean? Is it a serious threat?'

'I suppose one has to take all threats seriously,' she said. 'Don't you?'

'I'm glad you think so. Macarthy and Slater didn't.'

'You've seen them?'

'Yes. Do you have any idea why this is happening, or who could be doing it?'

'No idea at all,' she said. 'But it worries me.' She looked worried. Her cheerfulness was gone, her face crumpled like an anxious child. 'It can't mean anything, really, can it? Poor Leona was killed in an accident, you know that, I suppose? She was driving back to London from here. She'd spent the weekend with me.' She brushed tears from her chubby cheeks with a fist, then gulped her cocoa.

'Did she often do that?'

'Hardly ever. Once a year, perhaps. Sometimes twice, if I was lucky. But she always kept in touch, answered my letters, returned my calls. But the point is, you think this — person — put crosses by Leona's name because she was dead; but she just died by accident, it wasn't murder. So maybe this person's just going to wait for us to die, and be glad when we do, not actually do anything to us.' She looked at me quirkily, like a squirrel. 'Has she actually done anything?'

'How do you mean?'

'Well, nothing's happened to me. How about Grace and Melanie? Any clues there?'

'Apparently there's recently been a break-in

at Melanie's — her son mentioned it — but she didn't give me any reason to suppose it was connected to the Womun.'

'Oh, it must have been, surely. Too much of a coincidence, otherwise. Don't you think?'

'Perhaps,' I said. 'Ms Driscoll —'

'Elspeth, Elspeth, please.'

'Elspeth, what do you think women really want?'

'This woman wants more cocoa,' said Elspeth. 'Do you?'

'Please.'

'Good,' she said, bustling from fridge to stove and back to the fridge. 'I'm glad you dropped in for a natter. I always used to think I knew what women wanted, but then it all changed, because they got it. Sort of. In the late seventies and since. An equal go at things A proper job. No one telling them not to bother their pretty little heads. But Grace always told me I was class-bound. She said proper education and free child-care was what mattered, and Leona said it would all be all right if women were fully orgasmic, but that seemed odd to me because men have always been fully orgasmic, haven't they, and more men kill themselves than women. And Melanie wanted to get back at her father. Then she stopped trying, and married him. Children, I suppose. All women want children. I did myself, but it — never happened.' She crashed the milk bottle against the fridge door, and it spilt. She went for a cloth, and mopped up, red in the face. 'What do you think?'

I'd been trying to follow her pin-ball thought-processes. 'What do I think women want? Uh — I think it depends on the individual woman. If you recast the question as "What should women have?", then maybe it comes down to two things: economic opportunity and equal recognition for their emotional needs. But I haven't read Freud, so I can't answer the question as he framed it at all.'

'You're a post-modern feminist, then,' she said heaping sugar into my mug. 'Or perhaps a post-feminist. It's a dreadful thing to admit, but I can't tell the difference now. In my day we'd have called you a liberal. But I'm out of touch. Been out of touch for years. Did a lot of work for the cause until the early eighties. Published, too, in magazines, and of course I wrote my book.'

She gave me the squirrel look again. I shrugged. 'Sorry,' I said. 'I don't know the field. Tell me about it.'

She sighed. 'It didn't make the impact I'd hoped. Not very many people did notice it, though I was reviewed in the women's press, of course. It sold seven hundred and eighty-two copies. Not counting the comps.'

'The comps?'

'The free copies, sent out to reviewers, and of course my ten. And I bought in the remainders, when they were going to pulp them. I've still got them in the attic. You think people will want something, then they don't. Such a — disappointment. A betrayal, even.'

The pain still sounded raw. I wondered why: surely that's what happened to most books? It was hard enough to get them published at all, let alone expect anyone to buy them. 'What was it called?' I said.

'*Wimmin*,' she said. 'I thought at least some women might want to know . . . You can't expect much from men, can you? But at least the sisters might. Well, never mind. Grace liked it. She's a good judge, you know. She's got an Alpha mind. The only one of us who had. I'm like *Brave New World*, you know. I'm glad I'm a Beta.' She looked at me with fleeting anxiety. 'Sorry, am I being too cliquey?'

'Alpha — A, Beta — B, *Brave New World*, Aldous Huxley's vision of the future with people bred and conditioned to an intellectual class system,' I said reassuringly.

'Oh, good, I don't meet people much . . . And I've never met a private investigator before, and I don't expect they're great readers on the whole, although why not, come to think of it? You must all wait about a lot, watching people, and so on. Plenty of time to catch up with your reading. Do you enjoy your profession?'

'Very much.'

'Good. That's very good. And it's much better being self-employed, then you don't have the irritations and petty jealousies of working with other people. You can organize things your way, and that's very important if you're a good or-

106

ganizer with an orderly mind. I found it a huge relief when I started working for mysef. In a way. There are drawbacks, of course.'

'Drawbacks?'

'Well, yes,' she said. 'While you're moving up in a large organization, you have the satisfaction of being appreciated, and the knowledge that any good you do is amplified by the importance of the institution you're working for. You can change the world. In a small way, of course, but you can.'

'So why did you decide to go self-employed?'

'Ah well. Reasons. Things weren't easy. And I had a disappointment at work.'

Again, the pain sounded raw.

'What work did you do?' I asked.

'That's enough about me,' she said. 'So now, what are you going to do about your client? Keep working for her?'

'I'm not sure. She sent me enough money for a day's work and expenses, and I've already done that, so logically now that I've warned you all I should pack it in and get on with other things.' I watched her, wondering if she hadn't answered my question on purpose, and if so, whether she had a reason other than not wanting to discuss a matter which was clearly painful. She looked guileless, and hurt, but she was making an effort to speak briskly.

'But you're not sure?' she said.

'I haven't found anything out yet. Not really. And I don't like giving up, not knowing who she is and what it's about. So I haven't decided what I'll do.'

I didn't get out of there until three o'clock. We'd moved on from cocoa to breakfast — Elspeth made a great fry-up — and set the world to rights.

In between, I'd managed to learn little more about her. She was short of cash (the telephone had been cut off for non-payment of the account); she'd inherited the house from her parents (and hadn't touched it since, by the look of it, in the way of upkeep, though it was very tidy and very clean); she bred dogs (Kerry Blue Terriers — I didn't even know what they looked like); she wasn't married but 'friends visited her from time to time'.

I made good time through the deserted country roads. When I hit the motorway with its heartening signs to London, I remembered something that didn't fit. The man with the thong: he'd said something about Elspeth's place, that I'd hear barking, but not just of the dogs. Which suggested that Elspeth's was an eccentric household. Yet she hadn't seemed to me to be particularly eccentric. Childlike, perhaps. Open in her responses. Not many people would welcome a stranger after midnight, feed them and settle down to chew the fat. But not the sort of eccentric that I'd call barking.

She did have friends to stay, she'd said. Male or female? Barking or sane? There'd been signs of male occupation in the coats hanging up in the hallway off the kitchen, but they were just country-type coats, the sort that don't belong to anyone but are kept for people to wear when they come to stay. They could have been Elspeth's father's coats.

I hadn't gone any further into the house than that.

Had I just had breakfast with the Womun? Possibly. Her voice didn't sound like the answering-machine voice, but it didn't sound impossibly unlike either. That didn't rule her out, anyway, any more than it had ruled out Grace. And she was slightly off-the-wall, the kind of person who might enjoy little plans and secrets. On the other hand she'd seemed upset about the hamster, plus I couldn't see what she'd have to gain from the enterprise. I couldn't see what any of the three surviving Vestal Virgins had to gain. And I couldn't see why neither Grace nor Melanie had told me what Elspeth had so readily admitted, that the Womun was a legacy from their Oxford past.

Mahler's Fifth Symphony had reached the Adagietto. I turned up the stereo, pressed the neat little black buttons to open the electric windows, and blasted my way home to London.

Chapter 11

I'm not usually up at dawn unless I've worked all night, but it is a time of day I'm fond of in London. I left the motorway as the sun rose and drove through the almost-deserted streets, thinking that now, for an hour or so, the city would belong to me and the few thousands of real Londoners going to work or delivering milk or driving the buses, beginning the first steps on the treadmill that keeps the city going. Wordsworth was wrong. It isn't an animal or a person, with a mighty heart: it's a gigantic machine that needs to be driven by me and people like me. Not the visitors. Not the provincials up for the day or the City commuters in from their suburbs with their season tickets, or even the tourists that we should treat more kindly with their A–Zs and their affection for the Royal Family and over-priced marmalade and Genuine British Sweaters that are about as British as Tokyo because they're designed for foreigners in bright colours because foreigners don't like Genuine British Colour-Sense, which values shades of sludge. God bless their hard currencies and their soft hearts.

I stopped Polly's car outside my flat, and in the silence of the stopped engine realized that I was high on sleeplessness. What precise function did I have in this romantic fantasy? How many private investigators does a city need to keep going? Or television researchers? And when did you last meet a soft-hearted tourist?

I opened the front door, stepped on an envelope, and didn't register it until I was half-way up the first flight of stairs. I went back. It was addressed to me, in block capitals. I pulled my sweatshirt sleeve over my hand and picked it up through the material, just in case it was from the Womun, although if so she was using a different pen and style of printing, and carried it upstairs to my kitchen table.

I made a cup of instant coffee, put on a pair of rubber gloves, and opened the envelope. Two hundred pounds in ten-pound notes, and a slip of paper.

I'M DANGEROUS. TRY TO STOP ME!
The Womun

It was different writing. Either a different person, or the same person trying to look different. Either way it was another day's work plus change for expenses on an assignment I didn't want to give up. The more I investigated, the less sense it made. I liked that. Simple problems, with their simple solutions, were bread and butter. This was pure cake, even if, I thought, remembering the murdered hamster, it might be poisoned cake.

Meanwhile I could grab two hours' sleep, and the treadmill of the city could go right ahead without me. If I stayed awake longer, who knew what might happen? I might find myself voting for John Major or relocating to Little Snobbery on the Puddle.

Peter brought me a cup of coffee at eight. I woke up with a start; you do, with hot liquid dripping on your face. It wasn't deliberate, on his part. Just an annoying habit. He never concentrated when he carried mugs or cups, so there was often a trail of splashes behind him.

He was bright-eyed and smug and 'I'm awake and you're not'-ish. Presumably his blonde had been good value. He wanted to sit and chat but I snubbed his enquiries about Barty, bawled him out about gossiping about me with his father and drenching me with coffee, sent him to vacuum the living-room and struggled towards the bath. No running today.

When I came downstairs, clean, he'd finished the living-room and was making more coffee. I checked the answering machine: no calls. Damn Barty, why couldn't he just return my call? Although it probably wouldn't be difficult to locate him, I was reluctant to waste precious work time on it. Or reluctant to run after him.

'I reckon I'll finish the shelves today,' said Peter.

'Good,' I said, staring at my action board through still-bleary eyes What had I to do, immediately? There was the scribbled list I'd made last night of the names at the address in Harley

Street that Arabella Trigg had visited. I'd start phoning them a bit later, but I'd keep the phone free for a while to give Ready Eddy a chance to get through with his information.

Peter kept chattering on, asking me questions which I answered automatically, about my investigations into the Womun. Finally he said, 'It seems to me you could do with talking to someone who's known all these women at Oxford and since then, who can tell you about which of them is likely to be doing this, or who hated them when they were at college. That kind of stuff.'

'Good idea,' I said absentmindedly.

'Listen to me, Alex.'

'I am.'

'No, you're not. What did I just say?'

'You said I needed to talk to an old friend of theirs. And you could be right. It might be a hassle to find one, though.'

'Why don't you start with him?'

'Who?'

He waved his hand towards my action board. 'The guy who took the photograph.'

I looked once more at the Virgins in Punt photograph. 'How do you know a man took it?'

'Are those women dykes?'

'Not all of them, certainly. Maybe none of them. But what —'

'Then I tell you they're posing for a man. Listen to me, Alex, photography's my business. Those girls are smiling at someone they know well, someone they trust, someone they fancy.'

113

I looked again. He could be right.

'Plus, there's something else about it,' he said.

'What?'

'I'm surprised you haven't noticed. Look at the framing. Look at the quality. That's no ordinary happy snap. It's bloody good. Bet you that guy went on to be a professional.'

Which didn't, of course, help me at all. But his first point might. I added *?foto* to my action list on the board. Then the telephone rang.

'I'll get it,' I said, and plunged through to the living-room.

It wasn't Barty. It was a male voice, deep, young, almost familiar. 'Alex Tanner?'

'Yes.'

'This is Teddy. Teddy Webb.' Melanie Slater's son. I didn't know why he called himself Webb. Maybe that was his father's surname.

'Hi, Teddy,' I said, trying to sound pleased that he'd rung because he sounded so delighted to be talking to me.

'I want to come and see you. Would this morning be all right?'

'What's it about?'

'I want to hire you. As a private investigator.'

I hesitated, then I told him what I charged, not just because I didn't want to work for nothing but also because I wanted to make sure he'd thought his pretext through. I haven't much experience in dealing with adolescent males in the throes of a crush — I'm not obvious crush material — but I thought it likely that he just wanted

114

to see me. I wanted to avoid wasting time; even more, I wanted to avoid the embarrassment of an unprepared Teddy wriggling and waving his wrists at me in confused supplication.

It didn't faze him. 'I've got some money saved. Quite a lot, actually,' he said proudly. One macho point to him, I supposed. Perhaps he could show me his model Ferrari. 'It'll be worth it to me.'

'Then I expect we can do business. Aren't you at school this morning?'

'No, I've got a reading day, and I've already done the work, and now I've decided to go ahead with you I want to get it going as soon as possible.'

'I can see you at eleven-thirty,' I said. 'I've lots on, so be on time. And I'll expect a retainer, minimum four hundred pounds. In cash.'

He didn't gulp. 'I'm looking forward to it,' he said.

'Right,' I said.

Pause. Then, 'Are you?' he said.

'Am I what?'

'Looking forward to it?'

Hurt or lie. Just this once, Teddy, I thought, and after that it's every infatuate for himself. 'Yes,' I said. 'I'm looking forward to it.'

Soon after that Nick arrived, bubbling, her baseball cap on backwards, full of Grace. Peter made more coffee, fed the toaster, and they crunched through half a loaf between them — I wasn't hungry — and talked at me, simultaneously.

'So I'll get down to the shelves right after this,

should be through by six. I'm out with Katie tonight, right, Alex, you don't mind, do you? You'd like her. She's great, guess how she spells her name?'

'She's really kind. Unbelievable. Tad and Fred and me, and a painter in the basement but I didn't catch his name, an artist painter not a builder like Tad and Fred, and then there's her daughter but I didn't like her much, all in the same house. And a big dog that's going to be a guide dog for the blind when he's old enough. Grace is keeping him for a while so he gets used to people.'

'I can't guess, Peter,' I said. 'Gosh, Nick.'

'KT,' said Peter. 'Isn't that something?' He laughed. Teasing me: he knew my reaction to affected spellings.

'I hope she's got long legs,' I said. 'All the way up to her head. To fill the space more usually occupied by a brain.'

'And she's a professor at Oxford as well, and she's got cupboards full of awards for all the books she's written, and she gets fan letters every day, and she's got a great computer she lets me use, I never have enough computer-time, that's the only thing that gets me about being homeless —' said Nick.

'And I'm going to make a telephone call,' I said and shut the door behind me.

'Eddy? This is Alex.'

'Good morning, girlie. I was just going to call

with your info. One, forget Leona Power as a murder victim. It was an accident, straight up. D'you want the details?'

'Not now. Could you fax them to me?'

He sucked in his breath sharply. 'That'd be dodgy. Official information? You'd owe me.'

'OK, I'll owe you.'

'And the other thing, the alleged break-in at those premises in Kensington. Not reported.'

Not reported. Well, well. I'd have thought Melanie Slater would ring the local cop-shop at the slightest provocation, to boost the crime figures and get full value for her taxes.

'Aren't you going to say thank you nicely?' said Eddie huffily.

'Thank you nicely,' I said. 'Hey, Eddie. Tell me something. What do you think women want?'

'Ah. Well. Women. You've come to the right place.'

'Give me the benefit of your years of experience.'

'Go easy on the years . . . I'm happier with depth. Depth of experience.' He gave a salacious chuckle. 'All right, I'll tell you what women want. Plenty of TLC, a good seeing-to and a fitted kitchen. In that order. I try to make my excuses and leave after the knickers come off and before the brochures arrive. Get me?'

'I get you, but I think you're way off beam. That's not what *I* want,' I said tetchily. I usually butter Eddy up and swallow his opinions without argument — he's more like a sit-com character than a real person, and he's dead useful — but lack of sleep and lack of Barty was getting to me.

He whistled loudly, and I jerked the receiver from my ear too late. 'Ouch!'

'Serves you right. Don't get uppity with me, sweetheart. Remember who's doing the favours for who, right? All right?'

'All right,' I said. 'But it's still not what I want.'

'What do you want?'

I thought. Then I heard the voices from the kitchen, though I couldn't hear the words. 'I want to be alone,' I said.

'That's all very well when you're the right side of thirty and enough people don't want you to be. But remember what happened to Greta Whosit. She died alone.'

'So does everybody. And at least she was used to it.'

Chapter 12

Teddy arrived half an hour early, which threw all my arrangements out: I'd arranged for Peter and Nick to be ready to get out of the flat and leave me to speak to him in peace between eleven-thirty and twelve. He was apologetic, eager and compliant, though, which was just as well since when he turned up the flat was hardly convincing as the headquarters of a well-run private investigation agency.

We were in the living-room. Peter was sawing and hammering and singing along to Meatloaf about twelve feet away, admittedly behind a closed door, but a door built to rock-bottom specifications; Nick was in the kitchen behind another cheap door lying through her teeth over the phone to the receptionists of assorted medical practitioners who carried on their business from the Harley Street address Arabella Trigg had visited the night before; outside in the street, clearly audible through my open windows, the dustbin-men were arguing with one of my neighbours over the size of the bribe that would induce them to take away his bags of what was clearly garden rubbish, which isn't household waste, any way you cut it, so we'd be doing you a favour, know what I mean?

'I don't mind us talking here. This is fine, really, absolutely fine,' said Teddy. He looked smarter today: his hair was washed, and he wasn't wearing the tatty school uniform. He was wearing clean jeans, a dark grey polo-neck, an expensive, Italian-looking dark jacket, and a positive gale of after-shave. He'd taken a lot of trouble for me. 'I'm very grateful you agreed to see me at such short notice,' he went on. 'Alex? Are you listening?'

Peter'd asked me that, earlier, and I hadn't been, which didn't matter. But this did. OK, Teddy was only a boy, but he was paying, and the intensity of his crush was so evident it was almost painful. So I looked straight at him and tried to block out a dustbin-man's protest, 'A fiver? You've got to be joking!'

'Because this is important to me,' said Teddy. 'I want to hire you to find my father.' Then I stopped pretending and really listened, because this was probably important to him, and also because I wanted to know about his father: it might give me an angle on his mother. 'How do you mean, find?' I said.

'He disappeared. Nine years ago. When I was eight. He just went, and my mother didn't know where. Or she didn't want to tell me. I don't know what I thought, then. I missed him, of course, but I just, sort of — accepted it. Then a few years ago I was curious and I asked her and she wouldn't talk about it, and she's always refused to since.'

'Are you sure you want to find him?'

'Yes, sure.'

'Even if he doesn't want to be found?'

He shrugged. 'It doesn't matter. I might not even want to see him, if he's still alive. He obviously doesn't want to see me. But I just want to know.'

'Why?'

'Because I prefer to know,' he said. 'Wouldn't you?'

I approved of the sentiment, in principle. But I was also concerned that he might not like what I found. 'Why now?' I said.

'Because I saw him. On television.'

'Explain.'

'On the news, during the Notting Hill Carnival. I just saw his face, on a balcony near here, watching the floats go past. A few yards away, actually, on one of those big falling-down houses on the Grove.'

'Those houses are very valuable,' I said, rather miffed.

'Oh, I'm sure they are,' he said hastily. 'And lots of places round here are very cool. Much better than where I live. And your flat is . . . great. Terrific. But anyway, it was definitely my father. I think. Much older, of course, than I remember him. But he has a memorable face. Big. Lots of bone. Rather . . . ugly, I suppose. A bit like mine.'

'You're not ugly,' I said, because in those circumstances it's impossible not to, not because I wanted to encourage him. Besides, he wasn't ugly. Odd-looking. His face, still unset, would one day be distinctive, and attractive if you liked men craggy with long jaws and noses. Rather like Barty, in fact.

'Really not?' he said. 'Not too . . . bony? What do you think?' He leant forward eagerly.

Ouch. Thank God I'd never have to be fourteen again. It happened much younger to girls. Be kind, but not too kind, Alex. 'I think you have a very attractive face, Teddy.'

The smile he gave turned my sop into truth. 'So do you,' he said. 'And' — pause — 'so do you.'

At least he hadn't said it. Whatever it was.

We smiled at each other. For too long. He must have felt it, because he wiggled his hands and said, 'I've brought you a photograph.' He handed it over.

A family album snap. Written on the back, *Dressing the Tree — Xmas 1983.* In the colour photograph, Melanie Slater in jeans and a red sweater posing with an ornament and laughing at the camera, young Teddy in pyjamas grinning through the lower branches of a big tree, and an older, bespectacled edition of present Teddy in grey flannel trousers and a dark blue woollen shirt sitting glumly on a lowish sofa, large hands clasped around his knees, staring away from the tree and the camera, perhaps planning escape. 'He left ten days later,' said Teddy. 'Edward didn't like Christmas. That's his name, Edward.

Edward Webb, same as mine, except I've always been Teddy.'

'Was he married to your mother?'

'No. I don't think so. She's never been Mrs Webb, anyway. She was always Melanie Slater and she still is professionally, though when she married Nigel she took his name, of course, so she's Mrs Meades too, and my sister's Bella Meades and when she marries she'll be Bella something else. It must be peculiar, being a woman and changing your name all the time.'

'You don't have to,' I pointed out.

'Don't have to what?'

'Get married. Or change your name if you do . . . Teddy, who took this photograph?'

'Grace. Grace Macarthy. She'd come round for a drink and to drop off our presents. She gives terrific presents.'

'What kind of thing?'

'Oh, no particular kind of thing, and not always expensive. All different, depending on who she's giving them to. Never what she thinks you should have, but always the thing you want but didn't know you did until you unwrap it.'

'What did she give you last Christmas?'

He paused, and cleared his throat and said, 'Why do you want to know?'

'Just interested.'

'Well — OK. She gave me driving lessons, a course of twenty driving lessons.'

'And that was what you wanted?'

'Absolutely, because I was seventeen in January,

and then I could get a provisional driving licence, but —'

'But what?'

'But I knew my mother wouldn't let me. She has strong opinions about young people learning to drive. She thinks it's dangerous.' I'd have thought it more dangerous if they didn't learn properly, young. Maybe Melanie just didn't want an independent Teddy.

'So did your mother let you have the driving lessons?'

'That was the point of the present, not just the money. Grace can usually handle my mother. She out-argues her and . . . kind of bewitches her. So I had the lessons, but I don't really see what that has to do with it.'

Neither did I, yet. I looked at my notes and thought about what he'd told me. 'Teddy, the Notting Hill Carnival was about a month ago. Why haven't you hired a detective before?'

'I wasn't sure exactly how to go about looking for Dad. I came up this way a lot, I found what I thought was the house he'd been in, and I rang a few bells in the house, talked to a few guys. But no one knew who I was talking about, or said they didn't. None of them seemed likely to have known him. One of the flats was a crack house. It's a squat, I think.'

'Maybe you got the wrong house. Lots of them look the same.'

'Could be,' he said. 'That's your job, anyway, and I bet you're good at it.'

So I got down to my job. I made notes on what he could give me. He knew the broadcast he'd seen his father on had been the Sunday night of the Carnival, on the BBC news. ('My mother always makes me watch the BBC news. She thinks it's better than ITV.') He gave me the date his father had left/disappeared (Teddy remembered it because it was the day after his eighth birthday), and what he could remember about what his father did. He'd been a lecturer in maths, at one of the colleges of London University, Teddy thought.

'Did he go to Oxford? Is that where he met your mother?'

'I don't know,' said Teddy. 'That's not the kind of thing you know when you're very young, and afterwards my mother wouldn't talk about him at all. So I don't know much about him, except he worked alone a lot, sometimes on the computer, mostly just with pencil and paper. And he got into moods, and then they'd fight, and I think he'd hit my mother. She sometimes had a sore face. I mean, that's what I called it then. They were actually black eyes, I suppose.'

'How did you feel about him?'

'I loved him,' he said. 'I loved him very much. He was easy to be with, when he was in a good mood, and when he wasn't my mother kept me away from him. And he didn't nag me like she did. She was always there, all over me. She never left me alone. He'd show me things on the computer if I asked him but otherwise we'd sit in silence. He'd work and I'd — play, it was really — on the computer. Or else we'd play chess. He was very good at chess, I think.'

I was beginning to feel guilty about taking Teddy's money (brought, in cash, as promised) and it struck me that he'd have no real difficulty in handling the enquiry himself. He could press his mother for answers, or he could ask relatives or friends. There must be people still around who knew the story, and they'd surely feel that he had the right to know.

I suggested this to him but he shook his head emphatically. 'I don't want to do it myself. That's why I'm hiring you. I don't want to upset my mother, and any mention of him always does. Plus I don't know anybody who'd talk to me without reporting to her afterwards.'

'What about Grace Macarthy?' I said. 'It sounds as if she takes your side.'

He was taken aback for a moment, then said, 'Grace is terrific but she can't keep a secret. She's a very open person; she thinks problems should be faced and talked through. I couldn't count on her not talking to my mother about it, if she thought that was the right thing. She goes her own way.'

He knew her well; I, hardly at all. It had to be his judgement call, though I didn't think he was right. 'OK,' I said. 'I'll look into it.'

He grinned delightedly. 'Good. Soon? Now? I don't want to wait, you see, now I've made up my mind to do it.'

'I've got quite a lot on at the moment; I told you on the phone. Maybe you should get someone else.'

That was mean of me, since as far as I could see Teddy was paying four hundred pounds for the privilege of sitting in my living-room, gawping at me and doing his impression of an adolescent conger eel. He jumped straight in. 'Oh, no. It's got to be you. That's really when I decided to get a private investigator, because as I told you I was up this way and I went into your post office and saw your advertisement and I knew it was you.'

'You remembered me?'

'Oh, yes. I had a bit of a crush on you, actually. Back then. I thought about you a lot.'

'Thanks,' I said. 'I'm flattered. Hey, Teddy. You could do something for me —'

'Sure,' he said, interrupting. 'Anything at all. What can I do?'

'When I was over at your place seeing your mother, you mentioned a break-in. Could you tell me more about that?'

'If you like,' he said. 'It happened on Sunday night between about eight and ten. I was the only person in the house. Bella'd gone to stay with one of her whiny friends and my mother and Nigel had gone to a charity do. Someone broke in through the conservatory at the back of the house. I didn't hear anything.'

'Why?'

'I was in my room. It's at the top of the house.

I was working on my computer and playing heavy metal on the CD and I wouldn't have heard World War Three. Do you like heavy metal?'

'Very much,' I lied. It was simpler; I didn't want him to burn his CDs in ritual sacrifice. 'When they broke in, what did they do?'

'They went into the family room in the basement and smashed the television up and wrote on the walls in red paint.'

'What did they write?'

'I can't remember exactly. Lots of things. *Melanie Slater you must die* was one of them, and then stuff about women and babies. Bad stuff.'

He looked uncomfortable. 'Was it obscene?' I said.

'Sort of.'

'Can you give me an example?'

'Well, *baby-killer*, one of them said. My mother washed it all off quickly.'

'She washed off paint?'

'It was washable. It just went into being a pink mess, and then you couldn't read it, so I can't remember.'

He'd clearly decided not to tell me any more. Perhaps he thought I'd be shocked. Perhaps, although he knew the words, he didn't understand them.

'Was there a signature of any kind? Like "The Masked Avenger" or something?'

He laughed. 'That's kids' stuff!'

'But was there?'

'Not that I noticed.'

'Was anything taken?'

'No, nothing. It was just vandals.'

'The hamster was taken, of course,' I prompted. 'From the conservatory.'

'Oh. Yeah, yeah, it was.'

'When did it die?'

'Bella found it around tea-time. It probably died before then, but she found it when we were clearing up from lunch. We'd had lots of people over, we usually do Sunday lunchtime. My mother does a buffet and people drop in. Mostly invited by Nigel. He's a head-hunter, and it's a way of introducing people without seeming to, he says, and he gets it off expenses. And some of my mother's friends. Media people.'

'How many guests did you have that day?'

'Maybe thirty. I could make you a list, if you like. Why, does it matter?'

I couldn't press him any more without offering some explanation, so I didn't; I did want to know one more thing. 'No, don't bother. Teddy, did your mother tell you why I'd come to see her?'

He shook his head. 'She didn't say. It's to do with the book, isn't it?'

'The book?'

'Her latest. Coming out next month. Her usual stuff, what's wrong with contemporary morality, back to the fifties, all that. She's working on pre-publicity at the moment.'

'Oh, sure,' I said noncommittally. He sounded . . . contemptuous, I thought, and I wondered how much he liked his mother, despite his claim that he didn't want to upset her. 'Teddy, help me out on a project, would you? I'm asking everyone what they think women want. What would your answer be?'

'What do I think women want?' He thought for a while, popping his knuckles. 'You should know. Why ask me?'

'I'm asking everyone I meet. To get the broad view.'

'Marriage, I suppose. Security. An expensive house, with nice things.'

'Fair enough,' I said, writing it down.

'And you won't tell Grace I'm looking for my father?'

'No, I won't. And I won't ring you, in case I get your mother. I'll wait for you to ring me.'

Nick opened the kitchen door and popped her head out. 'Finished,' she said.

I called her in and introduced them. Teddy was quite different with her: natural, friendly, not at all self-conscious, and though Nick didn't talk much, she evidently liked him. I broke it up when they started discussing their A Levels, and walked him down the stairs to the front door. He turned on the step, with an open, appealing grin. He'd be very attractive one day. When he wasn't at the mercy of his hormones, he already was.

'Thanks, Alex,' he said. 'Thanks for everything. And let me know if I can help — about my father, or with anything else you're working on, anything at all.'

'I will, thanks. 'Bye,' I said, closing the door, but he held it.

'If I give you a proper answer to your question, will you promise not to mind if I say something?'

'Sure,' I said, puzzled. 'What question?'

'The question about what women really want. I think I know. Most women, I mean, not you, of course, or Grace. You're both different. But usually, women want to get inside your head. Particularly men's heads, but anyone's. So you can only think what they want you to think, and feel what they want you to feel.'

'OK,' I said. He had a point; I hadn't expected him to.

'And now can I say it? What I wanted to say to you?'

'Go ahead.'

'I think you've got the most beautiful breasts I've ever seen. On a real woman. Outside a magazine, and they're probably silicone anyway.'

What could I say? I stood on tip-toe to reach his cheek, brushed it with my lips, and shut the door.

Adolescence is a foreign country. They do things differently there.

Chapter 13

To escape the combined noise of the Black and Decker and Peter's karaoke efforts, I took Nick over to my local pub, the Churchill, for lunch. It's a cavernous place with dark brown carpets and pale brown walls. It used to be a drugs pub until the police raided it last year, after conducting a lengthy undercover surveillance which all the locals knew about and which severely disrupted the life of the neighbourhood. Now the pub is two-thirds empty and if you want to have a pee you have to get the key to the toilet from the barman, which is inhibiting. The dealers have moved to the pub up the road.

All the pub food is vile but the ham and tomato sandwiches are safest if you make them open a new packet of ham, so I ordered those, and a half of lager for me and a Coke for Nick. We sat at a corner table equidistant from the other two groups of patrons (four Irish builders and two pensioners), and I made an effort to give Nick some work experience.

'First thing: have you followed through with the vet about the hamster?'

'How do you mean?' she said.

'You were handling it. How did you leave it?'

'I said I'd ring back if we wanted the histology report.'

'And do we?'

'No. Not really, if it was stabbed.'

'So ring back and tell them thanks, party's over.'

'I was waiting for you to tell me what to do.'

'I was waiting for you to ask. You were handling it, so handle it.'

'I didn't know —' she began.

'Well, now you do. And don't make excuses, it's unprofessional.'

She opened her mouth to protest, shut it again, and swivelled her baseball cap so it was peak front.

'Second thing: have you told Grace Macarthy anything about the Womun investigation?'

She blushed.

'What have you told her?'

'Well — everything, I suppose.'

'Including that the hamster was stabbed?'

'Yes. We just talked about everything, because she was interested. She's interested in the whole world.'

'Never behave like that again. Do you see why?'

She shook her head, bit into her sandwich and made a face.

'And talk. If you don't talk, you're fired.'

'I don't see why,' she mumbled. 'Grace couldn't possibly have anything to do with it.'

'That's not the point. The point is, you're working for me. Anything you hear is confidential. You don't repeat it to an outsider unless I say that you can. It's called loyalty.'

'I'm not going to work in your stupid job, ever.'

'If you're a doctor it's just as important. Confidentiality for your patients. Loyalty to your colleagues and superiors.'

'You're bullying me,' she said.

'I'm not. I'm telling you. Because I think you're bright enough to understand, and tough enough to take it. And one more thing. You must not — absolutely not — get personally involved with someone you're dealing with professionally.'

'You keep saying "professional". This isn't a profession, what you do.'

'Any job's a profession if you do it properly and don't play at it. It's a question of self-respect.'

'That's crap,' she said flatly. 'My mum's job wasn't.'

'What did she do?'

'She was a tom.' I didn't say anything, and she explained. 'She was a prostitute.'

I knew that; I'd been running through possible answers in my mind. 'That's a profession too,' I said. 'Where did she work?'

'Paddington.'

'That's why you know the streets round there.'

'And the libraries. All the libraries. She worked in the daytime, she was too pissed at night.'

'Did you talk to Grace Macarthy about your mother?'

'No,' she said.

'Why?'

'I just didn't.'

Good, I thought. The prostitute mother was a useful sympathy card; I was impressed that Nick hadn't played it. It's the great temptation of abused or mistreated children, the way they learn to manipulate the world. 'So what libraries did you use?'

'The nearest was Porchester Road, of course, but the Marylebone Road one is bigger. So is the Kensington Central Library. And I like the one in St Martin's Lane, near Leicester Square.'

'What did you read?'

'Anything real. I hate stories. But mostly maths, because it was the easiest, and the most fun.'

'Not for me. You must have a gift for it.'

'I do,' she said simply. 'I'm a better mathematician than any of the teachers. It's not just me who says that, they say it too. And physics is easy, of course, and chemistry's not bad, and most of biology you don't have to think about at all, you just have to learn it. Which is why it's pointless me being at college most of the time. I go in for the practicals because I need to and sometimes I go in if the topic's interesting but usually I don't, and so I have a lot of time. I've always seemed to have a lot of time, and I don't like it. But I sort of know hanging round and going to libraries, so that's what I do.'

'Fine by me,' I said. I didn't mind her talking to me, if she wanted. It wasn't manipulative, or I didn't feel it so. I wondered, however, why she was explaining. 'Why are you telling me this now?'

'Because I feel bad about Grace.'

'Why?'

'Maybe I shouldn't have told her about all your stuff. Since I am working for you, and all. Maybe I shouldn't.'

'OK,' I said. 'Now you can tell me. How did she react?'

'To what?'

'Anything. Or, particularly, the stabbed hamster. Elspeth Driscoll reacted to that.'

'Grace didn't. I mean she didn't, any differently. Everything I said she kind of nodded and repeated to show she'd understood, whether it was about me or the case.'

'It sounds like a psychiatrist.'

'It's the same as psychiatrists, only she isn't being paid, so that makes all the difference. She's real and they're not. It's real people you need.' She paused, chewed some sandwich, then said, 'D'you want me to tell you what I found out about the Harley Street address?'

'Please.' She was beginning to self-start. Good.

'Basically, there are three sets of people in there, served by three receptionists. The first lot are oncologists.' She waited for me to ask, so I did, though I didn't need to. She was young enough for me to do her that small favour.

'Which means . . . ?'

'Cancer. They're cancer specialists. Then there's a load of physicians — obstetricians, paediatricians, endocrinologists.'

'Pregnancy and birth, kids, glands,' I said. She'd

136

had her thirty seconds of flattery.

'Yeah. And then the third lot are physiotherapists. None of them live there, though the physiotherapists are open late. Last appointment 8.30.'

'So what do you think?'

'She could have an appointment with a physiotherapist, for treatment. She could have been meeting one of the other doctors after hours, but not for treatment because even if they were prepared to make a special late appointment for her, none of them are the sort that you see every week for quite a while. No psychiatrists, for instance.'

'Hmm,' I said.

'So where do we go from here?'

That wasn't obvious. Not without Arabella Trigg herself finding out that someone was asking about her. If that didn't matter, I could ring up pretending to be a muddleheaded friend of hers whom she'd recommended to a physiotherapist whose name I couldn't remember, for an unspecified complaint. But Adrian Trigg had insisted she mustn't know.

'I'm putting the Trigg case on hold for a while,' I said.

'What did the kid want you to do?'

The kid? Oh, Teddy. Who was exactly Nick's age, and in some ways more mature. 'He wanted me to track down his father for him. Edward Webb. He disappeared nine years ago.'

'And do you think you'll find him?'

'I think he may well be dead,' I said. 'Anyway,

right now, you're back on the Womun. I want you to go and look this lot up for me.'

She read the list I gave her. 'That's easy,' she said, rather disappointed. 'They'll have this stuff in the piddling little North Kensington Library, right next door.'

'Next time I'll try and think of something more challenging,' I said. 'Something you'll need the Central Library for.'

Chapter 14

I was back at the flat at two o'clock. Peter had finished the shelves. He'd done a good job, too. And he'd gone out, and left me alone. That was best of all, because if I was to function effectively, I badly needed at least half an hour's peace, to drink coffee and think.

I had too much on. I felt like Charlton Heston in *Ben Hur*, a chariot-driver with three horses all pulling different ways. It's not a feeling I usually mind, because I'm an adrenaline addict. It's cheaper than other addictions but it can screw things up equally, because when you have too much to do, you make mistakes. And I was feeling as if at least two of the three chariot-horses could be dangerous. Not the Trigg thing; that would soon be sorted, and in any case it was minor. But Teddy's quest for his father was potentially explosive, and the Womun was a wild card. So far, the more I'd found out, the less I'd understood.

But first, I'd try to trace Barty, who was of course the fourth horse in my chariot, the ghost horse because I didn't admit how much he was distracting me.

I sat down at the phone and dialled his number. When the answering service woman spoke, I rang off, and dialled the number of the editing suite we'd been working in all day Sunday, before we ended up in bed.

Dave Marshall, the owner, answered. He's an amiable Londoner in his forties, a good editor and a supergood family man. We did the 'Hi, how are you?', bit, briefly because we'd seen each other so recently, then I said as casually as I could, 'Dave, is Barty there?'

'No. He finished the edit yesterday.'

'Right,' I said. So Barty hadn't gone away: he was still about. 'Have you got the number of his new mobile?' I guessed he'd got one: he had to have a phone which functioned for urgent incoming calls.

'Hey, Alex, what is all this?' said Dave uncomfortably.

'What's all what? Have you got the number of his mobile or not?'

'Yes, I do,' he said. 'Don't you?'

'If I did, would I have asked?' I snapped.

'Who's rattled your cage?'

I took a deep breath. 'Sorry,' I said. 'Giss the number, Dave. I'm a bit pressed.'

'No can do. Barty told me not to give it to anyone. He made a point of it.'

I laughed. 'Come off it, Dave. He didn't mean me."

'He didn't say who he meant. He said nobody. Which means nobody.'

I wouldn't get anywhere now, I knew. He's stubborn as hell when he's pushed. So I lightened up and signed off, spitting to myself.

This was beyond a joke.

I went into the kitchen, put the kettle on and updated my action list. When I'd finished, it read:

Melanie Slater's break-in? 'baby-killer'?
  ? foto
  ? Thong said 'barking'
BBC archive footage — carnival, Teddy's
  father
Arabella Trigg — shopping

I looked at the list while the kettle boiled and tried to remember what Adrian Trigg had told me about his wife's shopping habits. She dropped the older two children off at their nursery school every morning, and then shopped while the au pair looked after the youngest one, that was it. Every morning. How much shopping could a woman do? Still, I'd put Nick on to follow her tomorrow morning, just in case she bought something illuminating and wasn't just updating the shade of her nail polish or searching out rare spices to follow a recipe from the lifestyle section of her favourite newspaper.

I made instant coffee and took it with me to the phone. Ring, ring, answer. 'Jordan? Alex here. How ya doin'?'

Squawk.

'Listen, did you know the Vestal Virgins back

141

in Oxford? OK, no reason why you should have. Just one more question, then . . . The Vestal Virgins pic you used in the Leona Power tribute. Where did you get it from?'

Cough. Squawk.

'Macarthy? Right. Any idea who took it? OK, I'll ask her myself. Take care.'

Cough.

Ring, ring, ring, answerphone. 'You've reached Grace Macarthy [chuckle]. I can't take your call right now. Leave your name and number —' I cut her recorded voice off before she could chuckle at me again.

I flicked through my organizer for BBC numbers, picked one. Ring, ring, ring, answer. 'Maggie? Hi, this is Alex Tanner. Fine, and you . . . ? It's been much too long. How's Paddy? Oh, did he? With Caz? Oh, shit, poor you. Yes, she was always a major cow . . . Absolutely . . . Awful director. Couldn't direct traffic . . . I slept through her last doc . . . Well, no, I didn't ring to talk about Caz. I need a copy of the Notting Hill Carnival footage you used on the Nine O'Clock a while back . . . Have you got a pencil?' I gave her the details and waited while she wrote them down, then listened while she explained the paperwork involved and the price. 'Can't you just lift it for me? I'll get it straight back to you.' I listened again, while she explained what I already knew, that now the BBC was having to be efficient and cost-effective they spent their whole time billing each other for services, and the paperwork took hours.

'I'll have to bill someone,' she concluded.

'OK. Bill Barty. O'Neill Productions. I'll send an order round with my assistant when she picks it up. Will you have it in an hour? Right, thanks, take care, Maggie, talk to you soon.' That'd teach Barty. I had plenty of his headed stationery.

It only took a few minutes to word-process the order. While it was printing I wandered in to the spare room to admire my shelves, and work out how many books I could fit on them. Maybe I should move my American private eye collection in here and use the shelves on the stairs for the current stuff from the London Library. Which reminded me of Barty; the London Library subscription had been his birthday present to me this year.

At this rate, he wouldn't be paying next year's.

Restless, I went to the kitchen. The tiles behind the cooker needed washing. I washed them, thinking idly I was glad I didn't have to keep Elspeth's kitchen clean, it'd be a nightmare. But she managed it. Unlike Grace, whose kitchen was grubby, despite the fact that she probably had a team of devoted cleaning women.

But Elspeth had a tidy nature. The cookery books on her shelves were arranged in order of height; she had a cork-board with utility receipts and telephone numbers and shopping lists, arranged in rows. She even had one of those milk-bottle containers with a little arrow to tell the milkman how many pints she needed. I'd noticed it while I was waiting for her to answer the door, sitting neatly on the step, complete with rinsed milk bottles. Several milk bottles. Either someone was currently staying with her, or milk was the staple of her diet.

She'd told me she couldn't afford to pay her phone bill till the end of the month. Pity. I'd have liked to talk to her, since I couldn't get Grace, to ask her who took the photograph.

I rinsed out the J-cloth and hung up the rubber gloves to dry. And then I saw it, in my mind's eye. Elspeth's cork-board and the utility bills. Not the phone bill; just the gas and electricity, and, next to them, a space. But the gas and electricity were both accounts for information, not for payment: budget accounts, where you paid a certain amount every month to spread the cost.

I never use budget accounts because the utility companies get your money before they've earned it. But tidy-minded people who like to conduct their affairs just-so, and who aren't money-wise, often do. People like Elspeth. As she did for gas and electricity. So why not for the telephone?

I added it to my action list.

Ring BT — E.D.'s phone.

Then the doorbell rang. I went to let Nick in. 'Hi,' she said as she followed me up the stairs. 'I've got all the stuff you wanted.'

144

She was beginning to speak to me unprompted. She deserved a reward and I gave her one in the form of a set of keys to my flat. 'Thanks,' she said, and fiddled about under her sweatshirt, fished out a chain with a key already on it, and added mine, looking coy. I groped briefly for an appropriate response, then wondered why I was being so slow. It was Grace or Grace, of course.

'Did Grace give you a key to her house?'

'Yeah. Yeah, she did. And she says I can stay while I'm working with you.'

She sounded pleased about it. I was surprised she wasn't disappointed that a term had been set to her bliss. 'And then you'll go back to your foster parents?'

'Maybe. Or maybe back to the streets. But Grace told me, it's one of the secrets of life, always sell too soon.'

'Sell what?'

'Like in the stock market, and in relationships too, she said it's important to get out before you're thrown out.'

Experienced Grace, skilled in the techniques she must so often need in handling infatuates. Tell 'em early, tell 'em when they think you're perfect, when they'll swallow anything you say, and then it won't be so difficult to shed them because your firmness will just be part of the magic that is Grace.

'OK,' I said. 'Show me what you've got.'

She handed over her notes, and then the telephone rang.

It was Elspeth, profoundly upset, calling from a neighbour's phone.

Half an hour later I was stuck in the commuter traffic leaving London on the M4, with a pile of cassette tapes for the journey on the seat beside me and my running clothes, toothbrush and toothpaste in a grip on the floor. Nick was presumably also stuck in the traffic, in a taxi on her way to the BBC at Shepherd's Bush to pick up the Notting Hill Carnival footage from Maggie. After that her work was finished for the day and she could head for Grace Macarthy's.

I was happy enough to be on my way to Elspeth's. For the next four hours I had nothing to do but drive, and think, two of my favourite occupations. I could also listen to the radio and catch up with the day's news. I usually read several newspapers, to keep up with the current media inventions, and to store away the few facts buried under the candyfloss of gossip and fashion suggestions, but I hadn't looked at a newspaper or watched a television news for days.

So I inched my way along the flyover past the West London factories and out to Heathrow, and watched the planes heaving their heavy bodies into the air and heading for all the places I'd never been and hoped one day to go, on expenses. I half listened to an unconvinced and unconvincing Cabinet Minister explaining that the latest Government cock-up was actually a triumph of statesmanship, and wondered what Elspeth was up to.

Apparently, her kennels had been broken into; slogans were painted on the walls, and one was signed by the Womun. So surprise me. I'd half made up my mind that she was the Womun, and if that was so, one of the obvious next steps was to stage an incident involving herself as victim.

On the other hand she had sounded genuinely upset. Someone had killed one of her dogs, she'd said. I thought it was only one dog, though it had several names, as pedigree dogs often do. I worked on a dog-show documentary a while back and my notes had read like the cast-list of a Russian play.

Was it likely she'd kill her own dog? The way she dressed and acted, she was like the stereotype of a middle-aged woman who prefers dogs to people. But her dogs were a business; she kept none of them as pets, as far as I could see. No dog-beds, no leads hanging up by the coats, and most of all no dog-smell. Her kitchen had smelt of stew and disinfectant.

The Womun — whether Elspeth or not — evidently found no difficulty in killing animals. Perhaps she even enjoyed it.

But middle-aged women didn't usually kill animals, from what I could remember of the literature. Children in the early stages of a career as a psychopath did: usually male children. So did older male perverts who tortured large animals, like horses and cows.

The traffic thinned out past the Henley turn-off

and the voice on the radio changed to an economist explaining why the Public Sector Borrowing Requirement crisis would be resolved by a decisive move by the Bank of England to lower interest rates. He was followed by another economist equally certain that the same crisis would be resolved by raising the interest rates. I began to feel drowsy. I was short on sleep, and patience. I wondered why economists were paid three times what I was, and were never sacked for being wrong. As far as I knew. Maybe if I'd had an Oxford education like the Vestal Virgins I'd understand.

I opened the windows, groped for a tape and clicked it in.

The Eagles. Fair enough. I'd sing along and that'd keep me awake, and I'd concentrate on trying to get one simple thing right.

Who killed the hamster? Forget the Womun. Focus on the hamster.

Suspect Number One had to be Teddy. He'd been there the afternoon it died. He was a young male. He'd been entirely unmoved by its death. He resented his mother: 'women want to get inside your head'. He must resent smug little Bella: he lived with her; I resented her, and I'd only met her twice. If I'd had to listen to non-stop twee burblings about Mopsy and Hamster Heaven day in and day out, I'd have reached for the upholstery needle.

I was happy with Teddy as first murderer. But he couldn't be the Womun. It had definitely been a female voice on my answerphone, and Teddy's voice was unequivocally male, at times as near as Anglo-Saxon voices get to a genuine bass. Plus there was no reason to suppose that he knew anything about the Oxford activities of the Vestal Virgins — Melanie wasn't likely to have told him.

The open windows were beginning to chill me and I couldn't hear the tape for wind-noise, but I was still sleepy and I needed petrol. So I pulled in at the next service station, filled the car up, and entertained myself in the queue to pay by trying to count how many of the hundreds of objects for sale in the pay-station anyone could conceivably want to buy. Oil, etc., OK. But how often, mid-journey, do you want a dried flower arrangement? Or a giant pink dinosaur? Or a cassette tape of *The Best of Tom Jones*? *Was* there a Best of Tom Jones?

Next to the pay-station was a telephone box. As I left I turned towards it, turned away, turned back and went in. I punched in my British Telecom card, then rang Barty's number. A different answering service voice; still female, but much older. No, sorry, Mr O'Neill wasn't available. Did I want to leave a message?

Yes, I did. From Alex Tanner. Could he please ring me to clear up a misunderstanding?

Ah. The voice had a message for Miss Tanner, if Miss Tanner rang.

'I'm ringing.'

Rustle of papers. Clearing of throat. I read, for the third time, the prostitute's card stuck up behind the instructions on use of the phone. Miss Birchstern promised strict discipline, locally. Then the voice, puzzled. 'I'm sorry, Miss Tanner, I don't understand this message. I've just begun my shift and the paperwork was passed on and —'

'Why don't you read it to me?' I suggested, hunching up against the cold wind.

'It really doesn't seem to make sense . . .'

'Perhaps it will to me,' I said, blowing on my chilled fingers.

'It just says . . . no, this can't be right —'

'Give me the message,' I snapped, sounding remarkably like Miss Birchstern.

'It says,' the voice said huffily, ' "So find me. Smartass." '

Chapter 15

That did it. Of course I could find him, if I really tried. But I had other things to do than playing silly buggers with him.

Still, I'd have a cup of coffee and think about it. I needed a break from driving.

I reversed, bad-temperedly and illegally, from the fuel section to the restaurants and toilets section of the service area, parked and went through to the self-service café. It was almost full of people who looked, under the glaring light and through my irritable eyes, as if they were in the second day of a particularly debilitating attack of flu.

I took my lukewarm coffee to the furthest corner of the barn-like room and sat facing the window and the twilit motorway. Headlights streamed towards me and away and I tried to remember anything Barty had told me last Sunday about his planned movements for this week.

The documentary he was working on, about American aid to the IRA, was nearly finished. He'd said something about taking the shuttle to Belfast mid-week to see a contact about a last-minute update on the figures. He'd also mentioned lunch with the footling producer Alan Protheroe, a lunch he'd been putting off for weeks, and had been finally set for Thursday. Or Friday. I couldn't remember which, but I could find out.

Or could I? Barty was hiding. He'd moved out of his house, for sure. He'd be altogether too easy to find there. If he'd told Dave Marshall at the editing suite not to give out his mobile phone number, he'd probably have told Alan Protheroe the same. But Protheroe was bullyable. He did whatever the most powerful person told him.

On the other hand, he wouldn't find it easy to choose between Barty and me in terms of power. I was far more useful to him — I often worked for him and pulled his indecisive chestnuts out of the real-world fire — but Barty was a successful producer, not a mere researcher. And he was rich. And he was aristocratic. And he was a man.

No, I wouldn't risk approaching Alan directly. But I could certainly find out from his assistant where he was lunching Thursday and Friday, and put Nick on to it.

That's what I'd do, I decided, pushing away the coffee, which was undrinkable even by me, even after I'd bought it at motorway service station prices. Tomorrow I'd ring Alan's office, before he got in, and tackle his assistant, an amiable nubile idiot called Jacqui, employed for window-dressing.

When I arrived at Elspeth's house it was eight-thirty and dark as only the country can be. No reassuring background city glow: just pitch-black roads and brooding trees and a light drizzle to dampen whatever spirits the urban visitor might retain.

I parked in front of the house to a predictable chorus from the kennelled dogs, and before I reached the front door Elspeth opened it. She was wearing fluffy red slippers, dark grey flannel trousers, a white shirt and a thick matted wool sweater which might once have been blue but which had washed to grey. Her hair was sticking out from her head in fuzzy tufts and her face was swollen and blotched with several hours' worth of crying.

She hugged me and pulled me into the kitchen. 'My dear, my dear, thank you for coming. I never thought . . . oh, I never thought anyone would harm a dog. An innocent dog. My poor Gunpowder Blue, King of Kinsale. Poor, poor Gunny. That's what I call him — called him — oh dear.' She broke down into sobs, tore handfuls of kitchen paper and scrubbed at her face like a child. 'That — woman. I won't call her a bitch. I like bitches. I've never met a vindictive, heartless bitch, have you? Only human females. My poor Gunny. My best stud dog.'

'I'm very sorry,' I said. She was certainly genuinely emotional; she was convincing me. 'Which woman do you mean?'

'Melanie Slater, of course. Of course. The Womun in the Balaclava Helmet. I mean, it has to be. Only one of us three would know about it, would use that name now. Back in the sixties

153

in Oxford the Womun was a byword, but now everyone's forgotten, except us four, because people do forget, although you hope they won't, and then Leona died so there were only three of us left, and then when you came and told me about it I knew it wasn't me, of course, and so I thought it must be Grace up to some mischief because she does like mischief.'

I perched on a kitchen stool while she skittered round the kitchen in uncoordinated bursts of movement. 'You thought it was Grace?'

'Yes, I did. And if my phone had been on I'd've rung her to ask why and what she wanted me to do and if I could help. I'd've enjoyed helping; it's always fun doing anything with Grace. And I meant to ring from another phone but I never got round to it. And of course I was wrong and it wasn't Grace, it was Melanie —'

'How do you know?' I interrupted.

'Well, Grace would never kill a dog, would she? You haven't seen what that woman did. Come and see.'

She pulled me after her, outside towards the kennels, her fluffy slippers sliding and caking in the mud, still talking: 'I told the police immediately and they came to investigate and they sent people to take photographs and they asked me not to touch anything until the photograph people came, and it was terrible because the other dogs could smell the blood of course and they howled and I couldn't stop them.'

By this time we'd reached the kennel buildings

and the dogs weren't doing a bad job at howling her down once more. But as soon as she opened the door and spoke to them — 'I'm here, my darlings, I'm here, my pets, hush now, it's all right' — the din subsided.

Inside, I looked round, overpowered by the combined smell of dog pee and disinfectant. We were in a substantial shed, about thirty feet wide by forty feet long by ten feet high. On each side of a central concreted path was a row of dog-runs, fenced off with wire, leading to small covered kennels. Most of the dog-runs were occupied. It was a breed of dog I'd never seen before: large terriers, with long legs, square terrier heads and a short curly coat of a shade of black so dark it was almost blue.

Kerry Blues. So that was what they looked like.

They all ran to the front of the wire as Elspeth and I passed — she was taking me down the middle path towards the far end — and whined for her attention. But she was too absorbed to respond. 'Look. Come and look!'

As we approached the far wall of the building I could see writing on it in splashy red paint. *Kill! Kill! DEATH is what Wimmin want! I will seek out and KILL the betrayers!* And underneath it, the signature: *The Womun in the Balaclava Helmet.*

'He was here!' shouted Elspeth, stopping and pointing to an area of concrete splotched with dark stains. The dogs were howling again and I felt as if I was too close to the orchestra and

155

chorus in a Wagner opera. 'I moved him as soon as I could.'

'What were his injuries?' I shouted.

She began to sob again. 'That — that — that *bloody* Melanie cut off his head.'

Chapter 16

I didn't particularly want to view the dog's body, but Elspeth insisted. She took me into an outhouse, and there it was, on a low table, wrapped in a blanket. She opened the blanket for me to see.

Another Kerry Blue, in two parts. The neck had been severed neatly: by one blow, it seemed. The dark glazed eyes were still open. Elspeth put her hand forward and gently stroked its head in a tender movement which, more than her histrionics, convinced me that she had loved the dog.

Then something struck me. Its coat was matted with drying blood: she hadn't washed it. She hadn't closed its eyes. Why not? Perhaps the eyes wouldn't close because rigor had set in before she was allowed to touch anything. Or perhaps she wanted a shocking display for me.

She stopped stroking the head, patted the body and then wrapped it once more in the blanket. 'Come back to the house and we'll have some stew,' she said briskly. 'You must be hungry after driving all the way from London. But I wanted you to *see,* I wanted you to understand. She's really dangerous. You must take her seriously, you must, it's terribly important. You do understand, don't you?'

'I agree it's serious,' I said, following her back to the house and into the kitchen. I did think it was serious. What I didn't believe was that it had been done by Melanie Slater.

Nor did I necessarily believe that Elspeth thought it was Melanie, although she was trying to make me think she did. I felt manipulated. 'What do you think I should do?' I said.

'I'll have to think about that,' she said. 'The loo's through there if you want to wash your hands — past the coats, into the hall, turn left, under the stairs.'

I went. It was a small toilet, quarry-tiled, damp-smelling, but sparklingly clean. The walls were covered from floor to ceiling with championship certificates won by her dogs. The toilet seat was up. I put it down automatically. Peter never remembered, either.

It wasn't until I was buttoning my jeans that it struck me. Man-alert. Did she have a man staying there? Then I remembered the policemen.

She'd laid the table. Knives, forks, salt, pepper, Worcester sauce, butter, bread, two wine-glasses and linen serviettes. Plus a small vase of over-blown red roses, and two candles. Odd. She must be recovering. Or perhaps it was so fundamental to her to lay the table formally for a guest that she would struggle up from her death-bed to do it. Or perhaps she was in shock.

'Good, just in time,' she said. 'The stew's ready. I hope you don't mind mutton? Some people don't

158

eat it these days, but my freezer's full of it. Comes with keeping sheep.'

'I didn't know you were a farmer as well as a dog-breeder,' I said.

'Didn't I mention it? Probably because it's such a small enterprise. I only have fifty acres, you see, and I work it myself. Sheep, some free-range chickens, that's about it. Very stupid animals, sheep. Nervous. But good eating for me, though some people find mutton too rich.' She ladled stew on to two plates, put them on the table, went to the door to turn the overhead light off, and came to sit down.

She'd combed her hair and the candlelight was kind to her face. Suddenly, I could see the girl in the punt photograph lurking under the weatherbeaten flesh, and I felt sorry for her. Not because she'd aged, but because her aging had changed her so emphatically for the worse. I had no looks to speak of anyway but what I had would be with me until I was really old; I'd always look roughly the same, because I have regular features and good tough skin, and most of all because the lines of my face are straight, not curved. But her young prettiness had all been curves, and large eyes, and now the eyes were buried and the curves had sagged, and when she looked at herself she must see a different person.

'This is great,' I said, eating. It was good, too. 'Very kind of you. What time did the . . . break-in happen?'

'It must have been between three-thirty and

four-thirty. When I went out everything was all right in the kennels. Then when I came back I could hear the dogs howling, so I went in and found poor Gunny, and saw the writing on the wall. And then I was so — angry. Just so *angry,* and so sad, both at once, and I *really* hated Melanie, and I wanted to kill her.' She stopped, and gave me the squirrel look. Perhaps it had been seductive once.

'Do you keep the kennels locked?'

'Of course. Apart from everything else, the insurance company insists on it. She broke in through the back door.'

'How?'

'With a chisel or a crowbar or something, the police said. She broke the lock.'

'Did you tell the police you thought it was Melanie who'd done it?'

'No. And I didn't say anything about you and the warning you'd given me, because I didn't want to confuse them, before I'd spoken to you. But I had to report it because of the insurance, of course. Gunny is — was — a valuable dog.'

'Were the police helpful?'

She shrugged. 'What could they do? They were quite sympathetic. Considering he was only a dog, to them.'

'Did you have to give them pints of tea and have them hanging round the kitchen for hours?' I wanted to clear up the question of the toilet seat.

She looked at me blankly. 'Tea? No. I suppose

160

I should have . . . I was too upset. I didn't want to leave Gunny.'

'So the police didn't come into the house?' I plugged on.

'No. Does it matter?'

'Just trying to get the picture,' I said. 'Elspeth, I'm worried about leaving you alone, because I'll have to go back to London tonight. Is there a neighbour or a friend we could ring, to keep you company?' Surely, now, if she had a man staying she'd say so.

'I prefer being alone,' she said firmly. 'Some more stew?'

'Please.'

She took the plates, ladled us both a massive second helping, and sat back down again, heavily. 'I've decided what I think you should do. You absolutely must tell the police about the Womun in the Balaclava Helmet. About her threats. But I wonder if you should tell them about . . . us.'

'About the Vestal Virgins?'

'Well, you'll have to explain why we're the names on the list you got, I suppose. It was more that I didn't know whether you should say about us having been the Womun.'

I ate stew, and thought. 'But you think Melanie Slater is doing this, don't you? She's the one who should be stopped. In which case it would be much easier for the police to narrow it down to her if they know the full story.'

'I thought you could catch her yourself. Wouldn't you prefer that?'

'So why exactly do you want me to speak to the police?'

She mopped gravy from her empty plate with a chunk of bread. 'I'm not sure. I'm still upset. I'm very upset. And confused. I can't see things clearly. Help me, Alex. What do you think?'

'I think that if you really want the police to know that the break-in here was part of a sequence of threats, then you should tell them yourself,' I said. 'I'd like time to think it through, myself, and I'd like to speak to Melanie first.'

'Why?'

'Because she has a busy life in London. The chances are that she has an alibi for this afternoon, backed up by witnesses.' And I could find that out easily enough from Teddy, I thought.

'She could have found someone else to do the work,' said Elspeth.

'I suppose so,' I said, but I didn't believe it. Hire a hitman for a dog? I could see Grace Macarthy doing it, using one of her hangers-on. 'Tad, darling, just pop down to the country and top a dog for me.' 'Of course, Grace.' But not Melanie. 'Elspeth, do you really think Melanie's a dog-killing kind of person? She seems very . . . prosaic, very practical, to me.'

'I've known her longer than you have. And I know her better.' She stared at me defiantly.

'Of course,' I said. 'Elspeth, last time I was here and I told you about my client, you thought that it was Grace.'

'Yes, I told you that earlier.'

'I know you did. But then, today, you knew it wasn't Grace because she'd never kill a dog?'

'Yes.'

'But she'd have been happy to parcel up a dead hamster?'

'Yes.'

'Because I thought you were upset about the hamster, when I mentioned it.'

She looked uncomfortable. 'I was,' she said. 'It seemed such an . . . odd thing to do. Almost insane. And now I see it was. But you can never tell what Grace will do, except she'd never do something cruel. She'd never have killed Gunny.' She began to cry again.

'Was Gunny your favourite dog?'

'Yes. Yes, he was. That's what makes it so — brutal.'

'Could Melanie have known that? How much contact do you have with her, now? Has she ever been down to stay here, for instance?'

'Oh yes. We see each other quite a lot. We've been friends for a very long time.'

'And do you like her?'

'I thought I did. I do, but not if she killed Gunny.'

'But why should she?'

Elspeth had no sensible answer to that question, either then or in the rest of the hour I spent with her. I suggested that the Womun needn't be one of the Vestal Virgins, could be someone who'd known them since Oxford and had known

163

the alias, but she wouldn't even consider it. She insisted it was Melanie, but she couldn't or wouldn't suggest why.

And I still didn't know why she'd sent for me. Despite her obvious (and I thought genuine) distress over the dog, she didn't want my comfort. I didn't know what she did want, or what she could possibly gain from my presence. The one thing she'd asked me to do — tell the police — I wasn't going to do in a hurry, if at all, and I certainly wasn't going to name Melanie on Elspeth's say-so.

I pulled out of her gate at ten-thirty, drove back to Leadington, and parked by the village shop. It was closed, of course. What on earth did you do in the country if you ran out of groceries in the middle of the night? My local corner shop was open all night, selling my staples like bottom-range take-away curries and instant coffee, and running a mini-cab service on the side.

I looked across to Nelson Mandela Cottage. If there'd been a light on I'd have dropped in to ask Thong what he'd meant when he said Elspeth's household was 'barking' — whether he meant Elspeth herself or her friends — but the cottage was in darkness, so I looked at my map instead.

I needed to know more about the Vestal Virgins, long ago and now. I needed input from an outsider, urgently. One of the pieces of information Nick had quarried from the library for me was the name of the Oxford college which Grace, Melanie and Leona had attended. I assumed it was also Elspeth's, although she hadn't earned an entry in *Who's Who*.

A tutor of theirs would do nicely, if I could find one still in Oxford, still with all his/her marbles. It could be done on the telephone, but it would be easier, and more productive, in person. I'd stay the night at a hotel near Oxford and zap the college first thing in the morning.

It only took a minute to work out the route: Tewkesbury/Stow on the Wold/Chipping Norton. Good. It would take me an hour and a half, max. Three cassette tapes and seventy miles of unfamiliar roads later, I'd be presenting one of Barty's credit cards (serve him right) at an Oxford hotel. Heaven.

Thursday, 30 September

Chapter 17

I woke at seven. My hotel room faced south and the sun streamed through the streaky windows and picked out the stains on the bedcover and the chips and burns on the cheapish furniture. I felt impermanent, and at home. Before I got out of bed I reached for the phone and dialled Barty's number, just in case he'd sacked the answering service overnight.

He hadn't.

I rang off without leaving a message, put on my running gear and headed out through the deserted lobby and across the half-full car park into the crisp morning. The hotel was on the Oxford ring road, and as I jogged along the rough grass towards the city the commuter traffic was already building up.

It was ideal running weather: clear, sunny and spirit-lifting, but cool enough to go a distance. Five miles, I decided, and I'd aim for eleven-minute miles. Still not quite running, but not bad over five. I can manage eight minutes over three miles, but that is running, and leaves me knackered and wobbly-legged. My leg was broken last November and it's still not quite right. It will be, though. I'm working on it, because I don't like damage.

I was in North Oxford when I turned back: Morse country. That's how I know Oxford, through watching the Inspector Morse television series. Me and how many million others. I wondered, as I glanced in to the windows of the Victorian villas, which of them the production company had used for the exteriors of his flat. Cushy job, researching locations in Oxford. Every shot picturesque: can't miss. Plus the town's far enough from London to charge overnight expenses, pocket them and hop back to the smoke.

All the houses looked like Morse's. Street upon street upon street, all the same, smaller as you got further away from the city centre. Cost a bomb. Nice life, being a teacher here. Short hours, bright students, and one of the best libraries in the world. Paid to read. All right for some teachers.

Sorry, dons. Don was what they were called. I wondered what it meant. Latin, I supposed. I don't know any Latin, though I'm teaching myself Greek, on and off. It's a great language: makes a good sound, has terrific poetry. They say Latin's easier. Might try it some time.

The last half-mile back was a killer. Five miles is. I've never tried to go further. Maybe I should aim for eight.

Back to my room. Collapse. Then bath and dress, feeling strong. While the feeling lasted, I rang my answering machine and left a message for Nick. I'd already briefed her to follow Arabella Trigg's shopping expedition that morning. I needed to update her that I was in Oxford and would be back some time in the afternoon, and leave a call-back number at the hotel in case of emergency.

After I'd finished eating (full English breakfast, courtesy of Barty's credit card) it was still before nine. Too early to ring Protheroe's office and wrestle in mental mud with Jacqui. Time to visit the Vestal Virgins' dreaming spire.

St Scholastica's College was a massive red-brick building — no sign of a spire — on the border of North Oxford and Oxford proper, near the University Parks, at the far end of a wide tree-lined street now beginning to be scattered with rich red leaves. Although I couldn't see the river as I approached I guessed the grounds bordered it. Originally, I supposed, it had been an all-girls' college, but now the students coming out of the main entrance and disentangling their bikes from the long rows were about half male. Young, spotty, cheerful, on the whole. I'd be cheerful in their shoes.

I try not to waste energy on regrets. You can spend your whole life on 'what-if' and I can think of better ways of spending it. But some of the teachers at my school, particularly the head-teacher, had banged on at me about going to university. 'Possibly even' (awed emphasis) 'Oxford or Cambridge, Alex.' And I reckon I could have got in, even though the school had done its best to teach me the square root of sod-all.

But I couldn't afford it. I needed to work. It was a bad time for my mother; my last 'uncle' had just dumped her, she was in and out of the bin, and she needed me in London to look after her. On the other hand, I needed to be able to pay for a room of my own, otherwise I'd have been in the bin too. I couldn't just swan off and read. I had to have a marketable skill.

So I'd never gone to Oxford or Cambridge, and maybe it was a fantasy that I ever could have. How do you know how bright you are if you never run the intellectual hurdle race? OK, I thought I was cleverer than most people I met, but maybe that was just a sign of my stupidity. Maybe Barty's description was right; I was just a smartass.

I took my smart ass through the open gates and looked for the porter's lodge. The porter, a middle-aged woman (why not? they couldn't all be ancient male retainers) was helpful, and she didn't see a difficulty, even though I was asking about twenty-odd years ago. 'Now then,' she said, 'it's an English don you want?'

'I don't mind a foreigner,' I said.

'I mean, I think Grace Macarthy read English Literature. So you want a long-serving English don . . . Try Dame Janet Wilson first, I would. And you're lucky, she's in college already.'

'Is that unusual?'

'Quite. It's not term-time yet, of course. We're not even in noughth week yet.' (I didn't ask.) 'Go through the first quadrangle, as soon as you're

172

in the second turn left, up the first set of stairs, and her rooms are on the first floor. You'll see her name on the door.'

'Come in,' said the voice. I came in, to my dream room. Long, high, with wide windows overlooking the leafy quadrangle and the river beyond, plenty of low sofas and chairs, a long mahogany table, a desk, and every inch of wall that wasn't window covered with books.

I want it, I thought. Then I took it back. That was disloyal to my flat. I love my flat. Plus I didn't know how St Scholastica's was fixed for all-night corner shops.

'Who are you?' said the owner of the voice. She turned out to be an assortment of clothing apparently chosen, in a poor light, from a Laura Ashley catalogue, and she was sitting in an arm-chair at the far end of the room. The chair had also been covered by Laura Ashley, which was why I hadn't noticed its occupant, at first.

'Who are you?' she repeated.

'Dame Janet Wilson?' I said.

'No. You are not Janet Wilson. I am. Who are *you?*'

'Alex Tanner, Private Investigator.' I walked the length of the room and offered her one of my cards, which she peered at and then gave back to me. She was in her sixties. Even sitting down she looked tall. She was very wide, and seemed wider because she sat with her legs planted firmly apart. She had a big, bony face, a slight moustache and a bun of long straight grey hair tinged with natural yellow streaks, probably nicotine, judging from the cigarette between her fingers and the overflowing ashtray on a table by her side.

'What do you want, Alex Tanner?' she said, putting a pencil as a marker into the book she was reading, shutting it and putting it down on the table beside the ashtray. I looked to see what it was. If I read it perhaps I'd get her room.

No clues there. It was a John Grisham thriller I'd gulped weeks ago. She noticed me looking and said, 'Why do you suppose the Americans are so keen on books about lawyers?'

'Probably because they're obsessed with process,' I said.

'Perhaps you're right,' she said consideringly. 'And why do you suppose that is?'

'Because they lack traditions?' I suggested.

'Again, perhaps you're right,' she murmured. 'I had wondered if it were because the entire nation feels obliged to engage in continuous self-improvement, and the highest ideals they aspire to are professional. Perhaps, by "obsessed with process", you mean the same thing. But I digress, and we are getting into deep water . . . Sit down.' She pointed out a chair to her right. 'I am somewhat deaf in the left ear. Now tell me, what can I do for you?'

As concisely as I could, I told her the story of the Womun in the Balaclava Helmet. She listened without interrupting, until I described the break-in at Melanie Slater's. Then she said, 'Repeat, please, what was written on the walls.'

I repeated what Teddy had told me. 'I see,' she said. 'Go on, please.'

When I finished, she said, 'Extraordinary. How can I help you?'

'Do you remember the Vestal Virgins? It was a long time ago.'

'I recall the group's activities vaguely, and some of the pranks of the Womun in the Balaclava Helmet,' she said dismissively. Then her voice warmed. 'I remember Grace Macarthy very clearly, and I still see her quite often today. She has one of the most remarkable intellects I have ever taught.'

I wondered if you could separate an intellect from a person. Handy if you could. Send your intellect in to work, and go back to sleep. 'Remarkable in what way?'

She thought, then said: 'Clear. Quick. Original. Flexible. Wide-ranging. Imaginative. Sensitive. Perverse.'

'Perverse?'

'Not in any sexual sense, of course, although by all accounts she is sexually adventurous. Perverse in that she has an argumentative nature and will adopt any intellectual position in order to tease.' She sighed. 'Grace is a waste. She could have been a scholar. She chose merely to be a — a gadfly.'

'But she holds a lectureship at an Oxford college,' I protested, informed by Nick's notes on Grace's *Who's Who* entry.

'Indeed,' Janet Wilson agreed drily.

'Do you think she could be my Womun in the Balaclava Helmet?'

'Yes. Grace could be and do anything. If she chose to. However . . .' She hesitated.

'However?'

'However, she has never been, to my knowledge, of course, deliberately cruel, although she has probably caused a great deal of pain by accident, as she tramples through the lives of lesser beings. If, as you say, Elspeth Driberg —'

'Driscoll —'

'If Elspeth Driscoll was deeply upset by the death of her dog, I can hardly imagine that Grace was responsible. It is not like her.'

'What about Melanie Slater?'

'A good, solid, ambitious Beta Query Plus. Narrow. Very — female.'

'In what way?'

'*Kinder, Kirche, Küche.*' She saw my blankness, and translated. 'Children, God, the home. A German tag. Have you no German?'

'No.'

'I beg your pardon.'

'Not at all.'

'Can you imagine her doing any of this?'

'If a man asked her to. If she thought it would benefit her children.'

'Did you think her so female, even back then? She belonged to a feminist group, after all.'

'Only by accident. She is a hero-worshipper. At that time she was very young, and she worshipped Grace. And the young man she fell in love with also worshipped Grace, so they both served the cause.'

'Who was that?'

'I cannot remember his name. I never saw him, although during their Finals term I heard a great deal about him.'

'Why was that?'

'A most unfortunate business. I suggest you ask Grace to enlighten you.'

'I don't think Grace will enlighten me about anything. She's being unhelpful.'

'That's not like her,' she said thoughtfully.

'I don't mean she's been difficult. She's been charming. Just — bland. And uncommunicative.'

'Really. Well. Unfortunately, any information I may have pertaining to their Finals term is confidential. The most I can tell you is that all four of the Vestal Virgins were involved, in one way or another.' She looked pointedly at me. I was supposed to understand something, or do something, I could see. But what?

Keep asking, I supposed. 'Even Elspeth Driscoll?'

'Very much so.'

I thought for a few moments while Dame Janet watched me. 'This young man. Was his name Edward Webb?' An outside chance, but the only possibility I knew.

177

'I cannot remember his name,' she repeated.

'But you heard a lot about him. He was up at Oxford too?'

'Yes.'

'And involved with girls you were responsible for?'

'As I have told you.'

'So you probably had dealings with his college?'

There was a glint in her eye. I was getting warmer. 'Incessantly,' she said.

'Can you remember his college?'

'Naturally.'

'Which was it?'

'Balliol.'

'And who was responsible for him there? Who did you deal with?'

'You mean to ask for the name of his Moral Tutor,' she prompted gently.

'Can you remember the name of his Moral Tutor?'

'Charles Kinross,' she said. 'Once a fine mathematician, they tell me.'

'An Alpha Plus?' I said, trying for an Oxford tone.

I'd missed it.

'Not a classification I recognize,' she said frostily. 'An Alpha is absolute. But, yes, Charles was certainly an Alpha.'

'And now?'

'In his mid-eighties, and failing.'

'Is he completely out of it?'

'Intermittently. Better before the pubs open.'

Another pause, as if she was waiting for a Gamma undergraduate to haul herself from the shallows of ignorance to the rocks of certainty. Or perhaps they didn't let the Gammas into St Scholastica's.

I tried. 'Dame Janet, do you think it would be worth my while, considering what I need to know, to pursue this avenue of enquiry?'

She smiled. 'I have always wondered how one pursues an avenue. Surely by its very nature an avenue is static?'

And surely, by her very nature, this woman was a mischievous tease. No wonder she liked Grace so much. Or did she like her? She'd certainly made more effort to give me information once I'd told her Grace didn't want me to know. Competitive, that was the feeling between them. Probably a common emotion in a place where they seemed to spend their time sorting and grading each other's brains like eggs.

'Am I on the right lines?' I persisted.

'Another unilluminating metaphor. I have frequently —'

I didn't wait to hear what she had frequently. I interrupted. 'Do you think it would help me to understand what's going on with my client if I saw Mr Kinross?'

'129A Norham Gardens. Don't take him to the pub, and don't mention fairma.'

I didn't recognize the last word but I knew from her 'r' that it was French and from her tone that it was a joke, and since I didn't know what it was there was no danger that I would mention it. I did, however, recognize a hint when I heard one. 'Thank you very much for your time,' I said. 'Just one more question, if you don't mind. In English Literature, what is your area of specialization?'

'My field?'

'Yes.'

'Middle English.'

'So why are you reading John Grisham?'

She laughed. 'For the gratuitous sex. I always think the best sex is gratuitous, don't you?'

I laughed too. I couldn't help it, though I knew she was manipulating me. 'Try Sidney Sheldon,' I said.

As I left, she was scribbling in a notepad. It could have been Sheldon's name.

It could have been mine.

It could have been anything.

Chapter 18

Norham Gardens was just round the corner from St Scholastica's, the porter told me, and he gave me directions. On the way, I stopped at a BT booth and called Alan Protheroe's office. It was ten past ten; Alan wouldn't be in yet. I hoped. When Jacqui answered I asked for him all the same. 'Sorry, Alex,' she said in her high breathy voice, 'he's not in yet.'

'Damn,' I said.

'Can I help?' she offered with the air of one who, from long experience, expected the answer no.

'Yes,' I said.

'Oh,' she said, pleased. 'How?'

'Have you got his diary in the office?'

'Yes,' she said. 'It's on his desk.'

Pause.

'Could you get it?'

'Yes.'

Pause.

'Why don't you?' I suggested, feeling the minutes ticking away on my chargecard, and worrying about when the Oxford pubs opened.

'Oh, yes,' she said. 'I tell you what. I'll transfer the call through to his office, and I can talk to you from his desk.'

'Jacqui —' I shouted, but it was too late, she'd cut me off. Telephone systems weren't her strong point. Tits were.

I waited long enough for even Jacqui to have worked out that she'd cocked up irretrievably, and replaced the receivers to clear the line. Then I redialled.

Engaged tone. I hadn't waited long enough. Perhaps I should drop in to a showing of the director's cut of *Blade Runner*. Or marry and raise a family and ring back on my golden wedding.

I sang 'Hotel California' to myself, all the verses, twice through. Then I redialled.

'Alex? Is that you?'

'Hi, Jacqui.'

'So sorry. I must have cut you off.'

'Never mind.'

'I'm at Alan's desk now.'

'Good.'

'But I took the diary through to my desk. I'll re-route your call.'

'Jacqui!' I shouted, really loudly this time.

'Yes?' Puzzled little voice.

'I'm in a phone booth, and in a hurry. Just walk through and fetch the diary, OK? In case you cut me off again. OK?'

'OK,' she said. Silence. More silence. Perhaps she'd lost her way. No, I heard Marilyn Monroe-type breathing. She was back. 'I've got it,' she said.

'Brilliant,' I said. 'I've got to catch Alan today

or tomorrow, and the only windows I have are at lunchtime. Is he free for lunch today?'

Pause.

'Yes,' she said.

Oh, shit. 'Tomorrow would be better,' I said. 'Is he free for lunch tomorrow?'

'No,' she said. 'Barty O'Neill. Quaglino's. Lunch one o'clock.'

'Thanks, Jacqui,' I said. 'I'll be back to you.'

'Shall I tell him you rang?'

'Don't bother.'

I was safe enough there. She'd forget I'd called in five minutes.

129A Norham Gardens was a depressed-looking converted coach house in the overgrown garden of an overgrown Victorian villa. I couldn't find a bell, so I knocked at the door, and it swung open, revealing a small hallway entirely crammed with the tea-chests removal men use for packing. Was he moving out? 'Hello?' I called. 'Hello, Mr Kinross? Are you there? Is anyone there?'

'Come in, if you must,' quavered an old voice. 'Whoever you are,' it added.

I squeezed between the tea-chests and followed the hall through a sharp right turn into a smallish square room which, judging from the cooker, sink and fridge, was intended to be the kitchen, but which also held a table covered in computer print-out sheets and papers, obviously in use as a desk, and a camp-bed, on which an old man was lying dressed in plaid pyjamas and covered with a greying sheet and some stained blankets. He looked dirty and helpless and like a charity poster, and the room was indescribably filthy: used dishes covered with mouldering food overflowed the sink and were creeping across the parts of the floor not already littered with empty bottles. I did my best not to identify individual components of the almost tangible smell.

'Are you Meals on Wheels?' he barked irritably.

'No,' I said. 'Are you Mr Kinross?'

'No,' he said. 'I'm Dr Kinross, but you can call me Charles. If you buy me a drink.'

'I'm not going to buy you a drink,' I said.

'Why not?'

'Dame Janet Wilson warned me not to. If I wanted any information.'

'And do you?'

'Yes.'

'What about?' he said, heaving his heavy torso from the bed, swinging his spindly legs around and settling the blankets round him in a cocoon. Upright, he looked like Mr Pickwick, with a chubby rubicund face and a fringe of long white hair around a gleaming pink scalp. He was very old indeed. Even the stubble on his unshaven face looked soft, like a baby's hair.

'Information from over twenty years ago, about an undergraduate. You were his Moral Tutor.'

'What was his name?'

'I don't know.'

'You don't know?' He lay down again and turned his back to me. 'Why don't you go away

184

and check your facts?'

'His name is part of the information I want. Dame Janet either couldn't, or wouldn't, tell me. But we're talking about the Finals term of 1971. This boy was involved with several girls from St Scholastica's, in some trouble which Dame Janet won't tell me about. She says it's confidential.'

'1971? That is a long time ago. Why do you suppose I'd tell you what Janet won't?'

'She implied you would.'

'I'm not responsible for Janet's implications.'

'I know.' His back was still stubbornly turned to me. It wasn't easy interrogating a pink egg fringed with white fluff. Perhaps I should just get a rubber stamp and mark it *Alpha*.

'I don't want to talk to you,' he said. 'Go away.'

He was so childlike, I'd try treating him as a child. 'All right,' I said. 'I don't expect you can remember, anyway.'

'Don't have to,' he said triumphantly. 'I don't have to, because I never could remember anything except maths, so I wrote it down. It's all there.' He wagged a plump pink hand behind him in the direction of the hall.

'In the tea-chests?'

'Yes. I haven't unpacked them, but the movers cleared my rooms at Balliol. Including the filing cabinets. But I'm not going to look if you're not going to buy me a drink, so there.'

'Can I look?'

'No,' he said. 'Go away.'

'This could be very important.'

'Not to me.'

'I bet you don't even know which of the tea-chests it'll be in,' I said.

'Yes, I do. The one in the hall marked *Blue Filing Cabinet*. So there.'

'I'll buy you a drink.'

'Too late,' he said. 'Unless . . . no sort of mathematician, are you?'

Not in his terms, I wasn't. I didn't think an A grade at GCSE would qualify me. 'No,' I said.

'Pity. I need some help on fairma. I'm nearly there, you know. Got plenty of data. But I can only concentrate for short periods of time.'

I was no mathematician, but I knew a girl who said she was. I looked at my watch. Ten forty-five. Nick just might be back from her Arabella Trigg shopping assignment. 'Can I use your phone?' I said.

'No. Phones are expensive. Go away.'

'It wouldn't cost you anything. I'd use my chargecard. I'm looking for someone who'll help you with — fairma.' I wished I knew what the hell we were talking about. I hoped Nick would.

He turned round and sat up. His pyjama jacket fell open to reveal a chest covered with wiry grey hair. 'Really?' he said, as eager as a Christmas-morning child. 'Cross your heart?'

'Cross my heart.'

'Go on, then. Telephone. Now.'

I dialled. Nick answered. 'Alex Tanner's office.'

'Nick. Alex here. I need you with me, as soon

186

as possible. Take fifty pounds from the petty cash; top drawer, my desk. Go to Paddington, get the next fast train to Oxford, then take a taxi to 129A Norham Gardens.' I spelt it.

'OK,' said Nick. 'D'you want to hear about Arabella Trigg?'

'Not now. This is urgent. Tell me later. And bring any mail or telephone messages with you.'

'OK,' she said, 'on my way,' and rang off. Good for her. Very few people understand that 'urgent' can mean seconds.

'He's coming, isn't he?' said Kinross, lumbering out of bed. 'I must get dressed. How soon will he be here?'

'Not for an hour and a half at least,' I said, not correcting his assumption that Nick was a man in case sexism was another bat in his over-populated belfry.

'Never mind, never mind,' he said, moving about the confined and filthy space, crashing into things. 'That'll give you time to clear the upstairs bedrooms. And you might do something by way of cleaning in here. He might find it off-putting. We don't want to put him off, do we?'

'Why should I clear the bedrooms?'

'We have to have somewhere to sleep, girl. Can't sleep in here. This is the study.'

'Will he have to stay?'

'Of course. This may take some time.'

What had I committed Nick to? His last statement had a sinisterly permanent, Oates-stepping-out-into-the-Arctic-waste flavour. I backed as far as I could into the hall, to avoid his bumping into me. 'How long have you been working on fairma?'

'Exclusively, only ten years now. I've been toying with it since — oh, 1925, I suppose.'

Chapter 19

While I waited for Nick, I went to the nearest shop and spent nearly fifteen pounds on cleaning materials, including two sets of rubber gloves and ten ultra-strong rubbish bags. I'd been reluctant to leave Kinross unchaperoned during my shopping expedition — the pubs were open, after all — but he'd seemed engrossed in putting his notes in order in anticipation of Nick's arrival, and I'd risked it.

When I got back I cleaned the bathroom first, so he could have a bath, which he was surprisingly eager to do. 'Mustn't make a bad impression,' he said. 'I have rather let myself go. Do the kitchen next, there's a good girl. Throw away anything you like. Don't touch the table, that's all.' I did touch the table, of course; I had to search out the decaying Chinese food he'd scattered among the stacks of computer print-outs. I identified spare ribs in barbecue sauce and sweet and sour pork, but the rest, fortunately, remained a mystery. I tried to leave the papers in the same disorder as I found them. Then I spent an hour on the rest of the kitchen and did the best I could. A proper job would have taken a day.

I was putting the last of the four over-filled rubbish bags outside the front door when he came downstairs, spruce in a pin-stripe suit of ancient cut and a white shirt, apparently fresh from the laundry, ironed in fierce creases. Only the faint yellowing around the creases suggested that the shirt might have been waiting in its laundry packet since 1925. He was carrying two ties, still crackling in the cleaners' cellophane. 'Which do you think?' he asked, holding them up for me to see.

One was dark blue with maroon stripes. One was dark blue with emblems on it. I pointed to the emblemed one. 'That,' I said.

'I think you're right,' he said. 'It was my first instinct, too, but then I thought perhaps it was swanking a little. Bloody useless bunch of people, for the most part, anyway. Don't expect your chap thinks much of them. Academic societies give me a pain. Like the tie, though.'

I didn't ask. I was finding Oxford a place where it was safest not to.

'D'you suppose he'd like lunch at the Elizabeth? What day is it? Shut on Monday, the Elizabeth. Good enough restaurant, superb wine list. Always take visiting firemen to the Elizabeth.'

I wasn't letting him within a hundred miles of a superb wine list. 'Won't you want to get straight down to work?' I said weakly. I was beginning to feel guilty about his hopes. It wasn't my fault he'd decided Nick was the Leipzig Professor of Advanced Terra Fairma, or whatever he called it. I'd only said she was a mathematician. That was all I'd said.

But I hoped to hell she really was.

She arrived just after one. I watched her coming through the garden, baseball cap peak front, and my guilt ran riot. She looked like what she was, a gauche part-Asian street kid.

I went to meet her. 'This old guy's a half-dotty mathematician. He's got information I need and I think he'll give it to us if you play along with him about some maths he's working on. I said you could probably do it.'

'Do what?' she asked, not unreasonably.

'It sounds like "fairma".'

'Never heard of it.'

'Oh, shit,' I said, and for a moment I fantasized about taking Nick with me and walking out. I didn't want to watch the torrents of rain about to descend on his parade. And it was such a small parade. Not even a whole parade, just a senile float. But somewhere in his tea-chests was information Janet Wilson thought important, and she was an Alpha if ever I'd met one. I always try to listen when Alphas speak, though I'd never called them that before.

I took a deep breath. 'Do your best, Nick,' I said. 'Bluff.'

'OK.'

Kinross came out of the doorway behind us. 'Let me introduce you,' I said, as buoyantly as I could, and I didn't make a bad stab at it, under the circumstances: his face was falling as he looked at the female teenager standing where he'd expected a mathematician in his prime, perhaps a younger version of himself. 'Dr Kinross, may I introduce Nick Straker. Nick, this is Charles Kinross.'

Kinross looked no happier; he hesitated, then extended his hand politely. But Nick did. Her normal glum expression gave way to an enormous Cheshire Cat grin.

'Kinross!' she said, louder than I'd ever heard her speak, grasping his hand and pumping it up and down. 'It's . . . an honour to meet you. Sir. Professor. Doctor.' She was way over the top, I thought. Unless (could it be?) she actually recognized his name.

'I'm working on a proof of fairma,' he said defensively. 'What do you think?'

'I've never heard of it,' she said. He turned and walked away, and she talked on at his retreating back: 'I need your help.'

I tell her to bluff, and she says she doesn't know what he means? And now *she* needs *his* help? Perhaps it was something in the Oxford air. No wonder *Alice in Wonderland* was written here.

'Come on,' I said grimly, and followed him back into the kitchen, hoping to salvage what I could. He was bent over the papers on his table, looking suspiciously damp about the eyes. He'd be crying next.

I felt thoroughly pissed off. With myself for taking the outside chance on Nick, whose fault it wasn't, and for exploiting an old and foolish man. And with Janet Wilson for sending me on a wild-goose chase when she could have told me more, if she thought it important; or less, and sent me on my way without a time-wasting diversion into the Bog Kinross.

Nick went over and stood beside him. 'I need your help. On group theory.'

He shook his head. 'Read my book.'

'I have,' said Nick.

He looked at her with the beginning of interest. 'Found it difficult, hey?'

'Not at all,' she said. 'Very clear. Some of it was very beautiful. But what I thought was — I'll show you. Can I write on this?' She picked up a piece of paper from the table and glanced at it before he snatched it away and held it to his chest protectively.

'That's my work,' he said. 'Leave it alone. That's my work.'

'Oh,' she said, took out her notebook and a pencil, scribbled two words and held it for him to see. 'Is that what you're working on?'

As he read it, his face was once more a Christmas-morning child's. 'Of course it is. That's what I said. And you said you'd never heard of it.'

'I haven't. I've only seen the name written down. I thought it was pronounced *furmat*.'

I looked over their shoulders, at the notebook page. *Fermat's Theorem*, Nick had written. I was no wiser, but they were, gibbering away at each other about angles of approach and computer capacity.

'Can I look through the tea-chest now?' I said

loudly, but I had to repeat myself to get his attention, and then he made shoo movements with his hands.

'Not now. Not yet.'

'When?' I said.

'Oh —' He looked at Nick, looked at the table, looked at me again. 'Next week, perhaps.'

He wasn't getting her for a week.

'Tomorrow morning,' I said. 'Tomorrow morning, first thing, I'll come to pick up Nick, and you'll let me look. Or else we both leave, now.'

'Oh, all right,' he said, and sat down. 'Pull up a chair, Nick.'

Chapter 20

I left Nick to it. She didn't seem to mind: it was all I could do to drag her away from Kinross long enough to take her notes on the Arabella Trigg shadowing and to get her transcription of my telephone messages.

By two-thirty Barty's card had paid my bill at the hotel and I was on the road, glad to be heading for London.

I did the journey in under the hour. My flat was empty: no messages on the answering machine; a note from Peter said *Back at six — d'you want to go out to eat?*

No, I didn't, I didn't have time. I kicked off my boots, made a cup of coffee and ate the last of the Bournemouth hotel cheese. It was improving with age, but it needed to. Then I sat down at the kitchen table and looked at the information Nick'd given me.

Two telephone calls booking me provisionally for research work in November. Good.

Adrian Trigg: was I making any progress? Give him a ring, please.

Teddy Webb: how was it going? Did I need any help? He'd do anything I wanted. He'd be in Thursday evening and would call again.

Jordan: she'd remembered something about

Grace Macarthy that might be useful. If I wanted to know, call back.

That was all from the telephone. Nothing from Barty. Surprise me.

I went on to the Arabella Trigg notes.

1) Body Shop. Tried lipsticks. Bought nothing.

2) Principles. Tried two jackets. Bought one, light blue. The sort a television newsreader might wear. Paid in cash, eighty pounds (reduced from over a hundred and twenty).

3) Marks and Spencer. Underwear. Bought two dark-blue high-cut pants with lace trim, size ten, and two matching underwired dark-blue lace bras, size thirty-four C. Paid in cash, thirty-five pounds ninety-six pence. Children's dept. Bought light-blue trousers, for age four, three, two. Paid by cheque, thirty-eight pounds ninety-seven pence.

4) Cooks. Looked at long-haul holiday brochures. Took several, mostly Far East.

5) Boots. One economy-size toothpaste with fluoride, own brand. One giant family shampoo for normal hair, own brand. Five pounds twenty-three pence, paid by cheque. One large pack incontinence pads, own brand. One large box Super Tampax. Five pounds thirty-three pence, paid cash, different till.

I'd asked Nick for detail and she'd come through. Good girl.

She'd also solved the case for me. Incontinence pads. Unless Arabella was also shopping for her mother or grandmother. But it looked to me as if she was being treated by a physiotherapist for incontinence, probably brought on by producing three children so quickly, and she didn't want to tell her husband about it. Which was also why she'd paid for the incontinence pads and the Tampax in cash.

I went back to the notes again, looking for another angle. She'd also paid for other things in cash; perhaps she was planning to run away with a lover, wearing her new jacket and a change of lace-trimmed underclothes, possibly to the Far East.

A telephone call would settle it. I found the number of the physiotherapist practice in Harley Street, told the obliging girl who answered about my embarrassing problem, and said I'd been recommended to someone at that number but I couldn't remember his name.

'You mean Mr Spenlow,' she said.

'Yes, that's the name, great. Does he work evenings?'

'Yes.'

'Could I have an appointment next Tuesday evening? As late as possible. Say, eight o'clock?'

'I'm sorry, he has a regular patient at that time. I can offer you seven-thirty?'

'Oh dear. It has to be eight . . . Is there any chance your eight o'clock patient will cancel?'

'Not much, I'm afraid. Mrs Trigg is very reliable.'

Bingo. I disentangled myself and rang off.

That was Adrian Trigg's job done. I considered ringing him back and telling him, but decided against it. I'd write a report.

There was another note from Nick. *Grace says, do you want to have a drink and a chat with her at five-thirty this evening? She'll expect you unless you ring to cancel. PS. I didn't tell her you'd gone to Elspeth Driscoll's last night.*

Good for Nick. Again.

I rang Grace's number, let her answerphone message chuckle at me, and confirmed for five-thirty.

Then I rang Jordan. 'Hi. Alex here.'

Cough.

'You said you had info about Grace Macarthy.'

'You do a lot of work for Barty O'Neill, don't you?' she said.

'Yes.'

'He was up at Oxford with the Vestal Virgins. He had an on-and-off thing with Grace, before he married that beautiful idiot. And I'm not sure they didn't get back together again, briefly, after his divorce.'

'Barty and Grace?' I said blankly, trying to identify the emotion that was bringing the hotel cheese back up my throat and making it hard to speak.

'Yes. You can ask him.'

I thanked her, but not as warmly as she expected, and rang off over her protestations that I was an ungrateful cow.

But I'd identified my emotion. It was jealous rage.

I hate feeling jealous. When I was younger, I often did: jealous of girls who had what I hadn't, like looks and a home and a family and money and an education and a place in the world, so that their life was like a ski-jump, starting high up the hill and launching out into infinite possibilities, while I grubbed about at the bottom for enough of the necessities to keep me warm. It was a sick and poisoned and sapping feeling.

I'd been jealous of Barty before: of his ex-wife. Mildly. And that had been bad enough. But Grace. Amazin' Grace Macarthy, so pleased with herself, whose ski-jump had started so high up the hill. Oxford, confidence, and Barty too.

She wouldn't ever lose her nerve. She wouldn't have drowned the cheese-plant in wine. She'd probably have run through sixteen exotic love positions as described in an ancient Indian text-book (which she'd read in the original Sanskrit) before she took off her lace underclothes to reveal a perfect body. Even if it was a good fifteen years older than mine, it was still better.

I took several deep breaths and touched my toes.

I knew what I had to do.

I had to decide what to do about my Womun. Whoever she was. However many people she was.

And I had to work for Teddy Webb. I'd watch

the BBC Carnival video next; Nick had left it on the television.

But before I could, I went upstairs to the bathroom, vomited, and flushed the toilet on the last of the hotel cheese.

Chapter 21

I watched the Notting Hill Carnival footage twice through before I caught any faces on a balcony. When I did, I paused it. Several male and female faces. One of them looked something like the photograph of his father that Teddy'd given me. It could possibly have been the same man, ten years on; as he'd said. On the other hand it needn't have been. And the face was very drawn and haggard: it was perhaps older still. I supposed Edward Webb would now be about forty-three if he graduated in 1971. The face on the balcony could well have been in its fifties.

Teddy was right, though: it was the balcony of one of the houses on the Grove just round the corner from me, opposite the pub. It was very run-down: the police had used one of the flats in it for their drug surveillance. The others were, as far as I knew, squats.

But I did recognize one of the male faces on the balcony with the Edward Webb look-alike. I didn't know his name but he'd been a regular in the pub before the drug swoop. He probably drank in the pub up the road with all the others now. If he wasn't banged up in the Scrubs.

I could try him later that evening. After my drink with Grace. Which I'd have to leave for in half an hour. I wasn't going to dress up for her. Though I might put on a clean sweatshirt; maybe even the new green one, for jealousy.

Time for some more telephone calls.

I dialled directory enquiries for the number of the sub-post office at Leadington, Elspeth Driscoll's village. Enquiries gave me one of those interminable unfamiliar country numbers which probably double as the code for a Swiss bank account, and I punched it in irritably. If I'd had posh nails I'd have broken them.

I made a huge effort to sweeten up when the post office answered with a plump woman's voice. 'Hello?'

'Hello. I wonder if you can help me. I live in London but I was driving through Leadington and something went wrong with my car, and the gentleman who lives at Nelson Mandela Cottage was so kind, and I want to thank him, but I never got his name, and he really was so kind . . . and I thought you might know . . . Oh, Mr Drinkall, Richard Drinkall? D-r-i-n-k-a-l-l? Thank you so much . . . Because he was so kind . . . and so few people are kind nowadays, in London anyway, aren't they, so I did want to thank him . . .'

I was getting carried away, I realized, and rang off before she signed me up for a cake morning for the church roof fund.

Directory enquiries again.

Another Swiss bank account number.

'Hello?'

It sounded like Thong. After I explained who I was, he recognized me, so it was Thong. 'I wanted to ask you,' I said. 'You may not remember, but when you gave me directions to Elspeth Driscoll's place the other night, you said that when I got near I'd hear barking, but not just from the dogs. What did you mean?'

He spluttered.

'No, of course I didn't tell her . . . I just wondered what you meant, because I only met her that night but she seemed quite normal to me. I'm a private investigator working on a case and it would be helpful to know, in complete confidence, what you meant.'

I'd put him on the spot. He rambled on about a casual remark and not meaning it and having a high regard for Elspeth. 'I understand,' I said soothingly. 'I quite understand, but I also need to know. If you don't feel able to clarify, then I'll assume it was Elspeth you were talking about, shall I?'

'Absolutely not,' he said definitely. 'I was absolutely not referring to Elspeth.'

'Then to someone else who lives there, perhaps? Or often stays there?'

'Well — yes.'

'Anyone in particular?'

'Well — yes. A friend of hers from London.'

'A man?'

'Yes. But that's all I'll say.'

'So this friend is distinctly eccentric. In what way?'

'He's fought with everyone in the village, for God's sake. Not just me.'

'Fought physically?'

'Sometimes. He has violent rages. He's very strong.'

'Is he staying there now?'

'I expect so. He lives there, for all intents and purposes. And that really is all I'm prepared to say.'

'His name?'

'I suppose — oh, all right. His name's Edmund Wilson.'

I went into the kitchen for a mug of coffee and updated my action list. When I'd finished, it read:

Melanie Slater's break-in? 'baby-killer'?
  opportunity?
? foto
Edmund Wilson
BBC archive footage — carnival, Teddy's
  father — man in pub
? Elspeth's break-in — opportunity?
? delivery of Womun's letters — opportunity?
Ring BT — E.D.'s phone
Arabella Trigg — report

I looked at the list while the kettle boiled and tried to remember what was familiar about the name Edmund Wilson. I'd come across it in the papers, somewhere in the book sections. He'd written an autobiography, that was it. Full of spite and explicit sex. But what was he famous for? Why was he writing an autobiography anyway? And was he Elspeth Driscoll's unpopular house guest?

No, he couldn't be. The autobiographical Edmund Wilson was dead, because it was a posthumous work. I was remembering better now. It might even have been a diary, and he'd been an American academic of some kind.

I looked at the list again.

It's a commonplace of detective fiction that when people adopt an alias they often keep their initials. Most practical commonplaces of detective fiction are rooted in fact. So I crossed out *Teddy's father* and substituted *Edward Webb*, and made the coffee, wondering if I'd just earned Teddy's four hundred pounds.

No. It couldn't be that easy.

Ten minutes and one telephone call (pretending to be Elspeth) later, I had an answer from British Telecom. Elspeth had been paying by budget account until three weeks ago, when she'd cancelled the bank payment and begun an obstructive correspondence which ended in the phone being cut off. Her monthly payment was tiny: fifteen pounds. She must have one of the lowest quarterly bills in the country.

Don't tell me she couldn't have found fifteen pounds. She might have been hard up in her own terms, but she wasn't poor, not the kind of poor that couldn't find that kind of money. Her fridge had been full. There'd been a receipt on her cork-board from a clothes mail-order company that wasn't cheap. Besides, if cash-flow had been a problem, she could just have cancelled the budget payment and agreed to pay in full at the end of the next quarter; the woman from British Telecom had said, baffled, that that remained an option, and why didn't I take it?

As Elspeth, I hadn't answered. As Alex, I thought I knew why.

She'd wanted her phone cut off.

She'd wanted it cut off at a particular time.

Just when I started hearing from the Womun in the Balaclava Helmet.

As I brushed my teeth and changed my sweatshirt, I felt disappointed. I'd been looking forward to puzzling the Womun out, in my own time.

But if it was all being done by Elspeth Driscoll, I reckoned all I'd have to do was lean on Grace, tell her what I suspected and why I suspected it, and she'd admit that she'd known all along. She might even be able to tell me why, and that would really spoil my fun. *Why* was the salt of both my jobs: *why* was the brass ring. Anyone well-organized and thorough could find you *what*.

When I went out to the car it had begun to rain. The traffic was clotted up across the Harrow Road. I inched my way along, tried all the settings on the Golf's windscreen wipers and de-mister, and tapped my hand on the steering wheel. Fun fun fun. I tried the radio. Bosnia. I turned it off. I tried some cassettes: none of them were right. I groped in Polly's glove-compartment for more.

All I came up with was a large bottle of perfume. Mitsouko. Expensive. What the hell. I sprayed myself with it and groped some more.

Earrings. Large, dangly, jade earrings. I took out my sleepers and hooked the earrings in, and swung my head from side to side experimentally. The jade caught me a great crack across the jaw. I looked at myself in the wing mirror. Quite good. I'd keep them on.

The driver behind me was tooting. I'd missed a light. I turned and gave him two fingers, then repented. It wasn't his fault. He wasn't Grace. I gave him an apologetic smile and he tooted again, so I stopped appeasing and settled for concentrating on the traffic.

It should have taken twenty minutes. It took forty. When I parked outside Grace's house and got out it was raining really hard, bouncing up from the pavements and gurgling along the gutter. Most of the windows in the house were lighted; very few had closed curtains. I wondered which room we'd have her drink in, and how many of her hangers-on would join us.

I went up the steep steps to the front door, dodging the cracks and holes, and rang the doorbell. Then I retreated down two steps because a steady stream of water, probably from a broken drain-pipe, was drenching the door-step.

The front door opened. I looked up. Someone was standing there, back-lit, in jeans and a sweatshirt. Female. Built like Grace, but not Grace because she had short hair. The shadowed face looked half-familiar: a bit like Grace's.

It must be the daughter, I thought.

'Hi, come in, you must be Alex,' she said. 'I'm Fennel. Grace is my ma. She wants you upstairs, OK?'

I followed her in and up the stairs. Fennel. The early seventies had plenty to answer for, name-wise; she'd escaped fairly lightly. It could have been Garlic, or Basil.

Behind us I could hear Tad and Fred practising in the kitchen. Above us, the wailing of Billie Holiday. I thought we were going to Grace's study, but we passed it, and went up the next flight. Billie Holiday began to recede: her song was coming from the room next to Grace's study, possibly Fennel's room.

Now I could hear Abba, from above.

Another flight. Abba got louder. Fennel opened a door and stuck her head in. 'Alex, Ma,' she called loudly. Then she turned to me. 'Go on through,' she said. 'She's in the bath.'

Chapter 22

The first room was a bedroom. Quite big: about fourteen feet by twelve. Quite bare. A big low double bed, with white sheets and pillows and a white, possibly linen, duvet-cover. Fitted dark wood cupboards. A dark, polished wooden floor with sheepskin rugs by the bed. Small dark wood bedside tables, with Art Deco lamps that looked original. Very like Barty's.

A door to the right led to what must be the bathroom. Abba were singing from there, and steam was drifting out.

I looked at the bed again. 'Hi, Grace,' I called. 'How long have you lived in this house?'

'Twenty years,' she called back. 'Why?'

Twenty years. That covered Barty, before he married and after. Had the duvet covered him, here?

'No particular reason,' I said.

'Come through, get yourself a drink. It's Kir Royale or Kir Royale.'

'I'd like Kir Royale,' I said. What was it?

'Well, come in and get it,' she said in the sudden silence after the end of 'Super Trouper'. 'I never mind being seen naked.' (Chuckle.) 'In certain lights.'

I went in. A big bathroom, obviously a converted bedroom. A large corner bath, big enough for two people, now filled only with bubbles and Grace. Soft, pinkish light. Mirrors, a basin, a toilet, a bidet, a shower, and a long tiled shelf by the side of the bath holding piles of books, a cassette player now launching into 'Waterloo', champagne-glasses and an ice bucket with a silver flask in it.

She stopped the tape, reached for the flask and poured me a drink. I kept my eyes away from her body, took the drink and sipped it. Champagne with some sweet syrup base. Rather good.

'Look at yourself in that,' she said, pointing at an ornate brass-framed mirror in the corner. 'Over there.' I did. I looked terrific. 'It's the mirror from heaven,' she said. 'I found it in a junk shop in Camden High Street, years ago. I always look at myself in it, last thing before I go out. Then I know I'm beautiful. It takes me through.'

'Takes you through what?'

'Everything. Because I know when people look at me, that's what they're seeing.'

'But they're not,' I said, interested despite myself. 'Only you did, in that particular mirror.'

'What I see, they see,' she said. 'Great truth of life. D'you want to join me?' She swished water and foam over her breasts, lifted one long and elegant foot and waggled it in the air.

'No, thanks.'

'Why not? I'd have thought you were a bath person. That's why I asked you for half-past five, because I'm out to dinner at seven-thirty. You're late. I waited as long as I could.'

'Do you often ask people for drinks in the bath?'

'Yes,' she said. 'Why, does it annoy you?'

This was impossible. I was jealous. I was sick with jealousy. It was so bad I couldn't suppress it or distract myself or even concentrate on the work questions I had to ask her. All I could see was a happy, randy Barty beside her in the bubbles.

'Who is it?' she said.

'Who is what?'

'Who is it you're seeing? With me. Who did you see on the bed in there, with me, when you asked how long I'd had the house?'

'If you're so clever, can't you guess?' I said. I couldn't stop myself. It was game, set and match to her. I sounded like a spiteful child; I could hear it.

She chuckled. 'Sorry, no chance. I've been about a bit, you may have heard. Give me a clue. Is the person male or female?'

'Barty O'Neill,' I said. I know when I'm beaten. Mostly.

'Barty . . . When did you meet him?'

'Five years ago.'

'I haven't slept with Barty in the last five years, so you can stop feeling jealous. Unless jealous is what you like to feel. I'm jealous of you now. Not much, just a little. Barty's top of my list.'

'Top of what list?'

'Good men who got away,' she said. 'Now look

in the mirror again, top up your drink, take your clothes off, and get your ass in here, there's a good girl. You're missing fun. You're missing the Grace Experience. Strong men have killed for less.'

The Grace Experience was giving me a very soggy notebook, but she was right, it was fun. Sipping the drink, warmed by the bath and the bubbles and the entirely unsexual strength and warmth of the pressure of her long body, I felt exhilarated and weightless and powerful. 'Are you going to tell me about the Womun in the Balaclava Helmet?' I said.

'Whatever I can. It won't be much more than you know already. You ask, I'll answer. Watch your feet, I'm topping up with hot water.'

I moved my feet obediently. 'Do you think Elspeth is the Womun?'

'I *did,*' she said. 'I knew it wasn't me. I didn't think Melanie would bother. It had to be Elspeth, although I didn't know why.'

'But now you don't think it is?'

'No. I checked the timings with Nick. Nice kid, Nick.'

'The timings?'

'Elspeth couldn't have dropped the package off at your house last Sunday night. About ten o'clock, wasn't it? Well then. It couldn't have been her.'

'Why not?'

'She was with me. We both went to lunch with Melanie, left there about four, went to the cinema, came back here about eight, ate a takeaway Chinese and nattered until the small hours. She went home on Monday morning. How's your drink?'

I let her top me up. 'It still could be,' I said. 'How?'

'You could be lying.'

She chuckled. 'How true. But I know I'm not.'

'Or she could have an accomplice.'

'Sure,' she said. 'Who?'

'Edward Webb,' I said.

Silence. I'd surprised her. She flapped water over her breasts: a delaying tactic, I supposed. She couldn't hope it would distract me. 'Tell me what you know about Edward,' she said.

'I know he was Teddy's father. I know he lived with Melanie. I know he walked out, and as far as Teddy knows, he disappeared. And I think he stays with Elspeth under the name of Edmund Wilson.'

'Ah,' she said. A relieved 'Ah'? A delaying 'Ah'? I didn't know.

'I also think he was involved with all four of the Vestal Virgins, somehow, in your Finals term at Oxford.'

'Why do you think that?' she said.

'Because Janet Wilson told me,' I said.

'I don't believe you.'

'She certainly hinted at it,' I said.

'I can believe that. I don't think Janet's *told* anybody anything in her whole life. Not without irony.'

'Is it true?'

'Is what true?'

213

'Is it true that you were all involved with Edward at Oxford?'

'Yes.'

'Did he take the photograph of all four of you in a punt? The one you gave Jordan for the Leona Power tribute?'

'No.' Chuckle. 'That was taken by someone else entirely. Nothing to do with your investigation.'

Fine. I didn't want to get sidetracked on to her colourful past. I pressed on: 'Will you tell me what happened in your Finals term?'

'No. Most of it isn't my story to tell. And I won't discuss it any more. How's your drink?'

I held out my glass. 'What will you tell me about Edward?'

She thought. 'Edward isn't well.'

'How not well?'

'He had a car accident. Broke his back and fractured his skull. He has brain damage.'

'When was this?'

'When he left Melanie. He was depressed. It was a suicide attempt, I think. He drove his car into a tree. But not fast enough.'

'And Melanie didn't know about it?'

'I won't go into that. All I'll say is that Elspeth was living and working in London then. She visited him in hospital. Then she took him home with her. And when she left her job and moved down to Herefordshire, he went too. Most of the time.'

'Can he function now?'

214

'Within limits. I wouldn't have thought he could be anyone's accomplice, if that's what you mean. I certainly wouldn't use him, he's completely unpredictable.'

'Unpredictable enough to kill one of Elspeth's dogs?'

She was surprised — maybe even shocked — into stillness. 'When did this happen?' she said.

'Yesterday.'

'Tell me all about it.'

Grace was rattled by the dead dog. Not enough to give me much information, but enough to agree that she would speak to Elspeth as soon as possible and find out what was going on, and then tell me. She knew Elspeth's neighbours; she'd ring them and ask them to get Elspeth to call back later that evening, about ten.

'But you're going out to dinner. You'll have to come back early. Won't that spoil your fun?'

Chuckle. 'Not at all. I'll bring him back with me.'

'Can't you leave it till tomorrow?'

'No can do. Tomorrow, early, I'm off for the weekend. A literary festival down Bristol way. Readings, signings and pre-publicity for my new book. But we'd better have a contingency plan. In case I don't get her tonight. When can I reach you tomorrow?'

'Just leave a message on the answering machine.'

'But when will you pick it up? Will you be in tomorrow?'

I wondered at her insistence. Was she genuinely anxious about what Elspeth might do? But, if so, why did she have to involve me? Surely she could deal with Elspeth herself. No harm, though, in her knowing my movements. So I told her.

'I'll be out in the morning, back to the flat by about twelve-thirty at the latest, and then probably out again in the afternoon from about two until . . . say, six.'

'Right,' she said, and after that she wouldn't talk about the case at all. We talked about Nick, and Janet Wilson, and what it was like being a private investigator, and I enjoyed myself. Unthinkingly.

I caught a bus home. I was well over the limit for driving, and I wasn't going to risk my licence. Plus I like buses.

I'd been outmanoeuvred, of course. Grace had told me exactly what she wanted me to know, no more; and she'd charmed me, which was presumably what she'd set out to do. But unlike most charmers, she didn't leave me feeling ripped off, even as the champagne and whatever it was ebbed and left me semi-sober.

And I felt a lot better about Barty.

Friday, 1 October

Chapter 23

I was up and running at six. It was a dull, overcast morning; the sun was presumably somewhere up there, but it was losing the battle against the dense, threatening London clouds. It might rain, any minute, I felt as I breathed the damp air.

I didn't care. I felt wonderful. At one o'clock, Barty'd be at Quaglino's.

And so would Nick, with a message from me.

But I had plenty to do first.

By seven o'clock I was in a taxi, going over to Grace's to pick up the car. She hadn't rung the night before to tell me that she'd spoken to Elspeth. Maybe she hadn't managed to get her, or maybe she'd ring me this morning and leave a message. Whatever had happened, Elspeth was Grace's responsibility, for the moment, and I only had one bit of outstanding business in London.

Teddy Webb had rung back the evening before, while I was at Grace's, and left a message. He wanted to speak to me, urgently. He thought he could help me. He'd ring back at half-past eight this morning.

I'd hesitated over that. Should I wait for his call? I wanted to ask him something, too. I wanted to ask him why he hadn't mentioned, when he

219

told me about his parents' lunch party last Sunday, that Grace was there. We'd been talking about her, and he knew I was interested in the details of the lunch; was it just a casual omission? Or deliberate? And if deliberate, why?

But I was short of time. I couldn't rely on getting down to Oxford and back in time for lunch if I hung about in London until half-past eight.

So I was on my way to pick up Nick, with a hammer and screwdriver to open Kinross's tea-chest, and a competitive desire to find out what Grace was so determined to conceal from me about the Finals term, 1971.

I paid off the taxi and looked up at Grace's house. Most of the curtains were drawn. As I watched, Fennel came to a first-floor window and opened it. She must just have got out of bed; she was wearing a long T-shirt and she looked young, and sulky. Probably she wasn't a morning person.

I looked away before she noticed me, and unlocked the car. I must be getting old, I thought as I started up and drove away. All young people were beginning to look alike to me. Fennel looked a little like Nick: the same long face. And both of them looked like Teddy.

I made good time to Oxford until I had to slow down for Summertown, and then it was only ten minutes to Norham Gardens. Nick opened the door to me, and went straight back to the table to work at the computer print-outs. There were much fewer of them on the table, now. Kinross, still in his suit, was asleep on the camp bed in the corner. The remains of last night's Chinese takeaway were stacked neatly on the draining-board, with two empty litre bottles of Strongbow beside them.

'Nick — come and help me,' I said, fishing out the hammer and screwdriver from my bag. 'I want this information, and it'll be quieter if we open the tea-chest together.'

She shook her head without looking up. 'Uh-uh,' she said. 'He won't wake. I think his liver's shot. A little Strongbow and he was well gone. I want to finish this. He has some computer-time later today, and I've got to plot the program.'

I could have asked her who she thought she was working for, but why bother? I knew the answer.

I heaved the *Blue Filing Cabinet* tea-chest from the hall into the kitchen and started levering away at the nails on the lid. 'Did you get any sleep?' I said.

'Sleep?' she asked, astonished.

'Any chance of a cup of coffee?'

'Forget it,' she said. 'This is the most exciting thing that's happened to me. Ever. In my whole life.'

Two nails out, eight to go. The screwdriver slipped and gashed my left hand. 'Ouch,' I said. 'More exciting than Grace?'

'Do shut up,' she said. 'I'm working.'

I sucked the blood from my hand and kept levering. I was working, too.

The last nail was the hardest. They always are. But finally I removed the lid, propped it against the wall, and looked in. Stacks of old green filing cabinet suspension folders, still labelled with their little plastic tabs. I took them all out and sorted them in piles. *Wine Committee. Appointment of Master Steering Committee. Proceedings of the Royal Society. Fellowships, Awards and Prizes.* I flicked through those, curious. He'd collected them like beermats. Including a share of the Nobel Prize, in the fifties.

'Nick, he got the Nobel Prize for Physics!' I said.

'Did he?' she said.

'What do you suppose it was for?'

'His work on group theory, I expect. Or vector spaces. I don't know the physical applications. Do shut up.'

I looked at the pink and white old man on the bed, gently snuffling in his cider coma. 'They should look after him better. They should treat him with respect.'

'They do,' she said. 'They give him computer-time. Now if you don't shut up I'll have to move upstairs.'

The last set of files were the ones I was after. *Undergraduate Moral Tutees. 1945–1948.* I looked inside that one to check that the last date was the graduation date: it was. Flick, flick, flick. *1968–1971.* Got it.

I pulled the file out, looked at Nick, whose whole body was quivering with concentration, and took it outside to the car. I don't think she noticed me go.

Within the file, there were subdivisions by name, arranged alphabetically. Five names. No Webb.

Shit!

No Webb. But there was an O'Neill, Bartholomew.

Barty. Now I scratched around in my memory, I dimly recalled that he'd read Maths at Balliol. And he would have graduated in 1971; that made sense.

It was strange, holding three years of his life in my hand. Should I look?

Of course I shouldn't. This was confidential.

Of course I did.

There wasn't anything much. A complaint from the Proctors (who were they?) that he was involved in a drunken incident and hit a Bulldog (what was that?). The Bulldog was evidently human, because he was called Herbert Evans and he'd suffered contusions to the right cheek-bone.

Apart from that offence, for which he'd been gated for three weeks, Barty hadn't done much. There were complaints from the Deans of four of the women's colleges of his being found in their precincts after hours. On the iceberg principle I assumed that he'd spent most of his nights chasing tail and only been caught four times. Not bad. It was a retrospective comfort that most of

223

the women involved probably now looked like Elspeth Driscoll.

Although at least one of them still looked like Grace Macarthy.

I shut Barty's file on the information that he'd added a First in Schools to his amatory achievements, and thought about Webb.

It had to be Webb. It had to be. So why wasn't he here?

I took the file back indoors. Kinross had turned over, but he was still out of it. Nick was smiling as she scribbled, and she didn't notice me come in.

Back to the heaps of files. Webb must have been reclassified. Why?

If he went on to graduate work, perhaps. He'd ended up a lecturer at London University so he must have done a doctorate.

Graduate Supervisees was another classification. These were much slimmer and had open-ended dates, like *1950–* , presumably because it took varying lengths of time to complete the work. I found *1971–* and took it to the car, superstitiously not opening it before I sat down and closed the door.

Two names. *Zhukov.* And *Webb.*

Got it!

I read enough to check that the undergraduate file was included, and then headed for the nearest photocopying machine I knew of, in a Prontaprint in Summertown.

I parked illegally, dashed in and handed over

the Webb file for copying.

Time was running out. I had to be back in Central London for lunch, with or without Nick.

Chapter 24

It had to be without Nick. She wouldn't come. I packed the files back into the tea-chest, checked that she had enough money for a day or two, copied Kinross's number from his telephone, and left. I said goodbye to them both. Kinross was still comatose and I got no response from Nick either.

I made good enough time back to London to reach Shepherd's Bush by quarter to twelve, so I went back to the flat to change. If I was going to Quaglino's myself I wanted to look posh enough not to be shown the tradesmen's entrance. I'd go for broke and borrow something of Polly's.

On the mat just inside the front door there was an envelope. Addressed to me, in printed letters.

The Womun again. I stuffed it in my bag, unopened, between the hammer and the photocopies of Edward Webb's file. I'd read it later. I had the nagged-at, I've-been-responsive-long-enough feeling that comes from dealing with an attention-seeking child.

Up the stairs; into my flat for Polly's keys. No Peter. No messages on the answering machine, but a note propped up beside it.

11.30 A.M. *Friday. Sorry, spilt coffee on the an-*

safone and wrecked the tape. Think you lost three messages. Hope one of them wasn't last-minute call for six weeks' work starting tomorrow. Have put new tape in. Back nineish tonite. Love, P.

Probably one of those messages was Grace's. Couldn't be helped. I checked the carpet near the machine for coffee-stains, but there were none visible.

I had to hurry. Down again to Polly's flat below, into her bedroom and into the walk-in cupboard. I'd wear my own leggings. What I needed from her was a scoop-neck Lycra top and a drop-dead jacket.

I was spoilt for choice. And this was what Polly had left behind; she'd taken so much luggage with her that she'd had to pay overweight on the flight, even with her first-class baggage allowance. I stopped myself calculating how much money was hanging in her wardrobe. And how much interest it would earn, if it was invested, instead of just hanging here smelling faintly of Mitsouko.

In a good cause, I thought, riffling through the jackets, picking a narrow-cut, long, bright green, crumpled linen one. Polly wouldn't mind. She'd been pushing me at Barty for years. I didn't even feel guilty when I saw the label on the jacket I'd chosen. Armani.

I showered quickly, brushed my teeth and moussed my hair, put on a Janet Reger black lace underwired bra Polly'd given me last Christmas, and squeezed my size twelve torso into her size ten Lycra top. Must remember not to lean forward, or breathe too deeply. Pants. Leggings. Looked at myself. Leggings off. Pants off. Leggings on again. Better line.

I couldn't wear my Docs. Pity. I feel safer rough-shod. I wasn't going to cripple myself, though, so I compromised on a pair of patent-leather flatties Polly'd given me last birthday.

Now the jacket. Longer on me than on Polly, of course, but that helped my thighs: they're meaty. Grace's magic mirror might show them as voluptuous, but I knew they were meaty.

Jade earrings. Must remember not to move my head too quickly or I'd be in Casualty with a broken jaw.

I stepped back so I could see all of myself in the mirror.

It was good. It was as good as it could be.

Geronimo, then.

I clattered downstairs and checked the time. Twelve-thirty. Good. I could get over to Quaglino's, park, and swan in a quarter of an hour after Alan and Barty arrived.

I'd have to take a bag. The jacket was designed without pockets, presumably for women who were always followed by retainers with credit cards and money and keys. Or perhaps for women who merely turned to the man beside them and murmured their thanks.

I could borrow a bag of Polly's.

No, I'd just take my own. Drop-dead gorgeous, but casual, that was me.

I found a parking-meter straight away; not far from Quaglino's, either. It was definitely my day. I fed the meter and got back in the car. It was only five to one. Alan would arrive dead on time, Barty seven minutes late. The seven minutes of protocol, he'd once said. I hadn't known what he meant and I hadn't wanted to give him the satisfaction of asking.

That was a long time ago, though, when I still thought him snobbish, because his brother was an earl. He's actually one of the least snobbish men I know. But I could count on the seven minutes, for him. So I'd wait till they'd both arrived, then I'd go up.

I settled down to watch. Another routine surveillance. A few minutes went by. Alan should be here any time now. I checked my face in the rear-view mirror. Not bad. Liked the earrings.

Kept watching. Alan was now three minutes late. I fiddled with the Lycra top, reinserting most of what the push-up bra was pushing up, and smiling briefly as I remembered Teddy.

This was ridiculous. Good presentation was one thing, self-obsession another. I needed a distraction.

Still watching the street, I fished around in my bag for the Womun's letter, found it, and opened it.

I WILL SMASH THE GLASS CEILING THEY WILL SUFFER

*THEY DID NOT ACKNOWLEDGE ME
  THEN
NOW THEY MUST
AT ONE-THIRTY TODAY, FRIDAY
THEY WILL LIFT THEIR BLIND EYES
  AND SEE
BUT NOT FOR LONG —
UNLESS YOU STOP ME.*

I half read it once, my eyes on the street.

Then I read it again, with all my attention. I remembered Peter asking about the first letter, 'Where's this glass ceiling, then?' and me patronizing him: 'It's not a thing or a place, it's a feminist idea.'

I'd been wrong. As Freud said, sometimes a cigar is just a cigar.

And it was now ten past one. I had twenty minutes to get there, and stop her.

Get where?

And did I need to stop her?

Yes, if I could. Glass ceilings were potentially lethal. I couldn't risk the casualty list moving up from rodents through dogs to people. Plus she obviously expected me to. Was counting on it. But why hadn't she told me where?

Then it hit me. She probably had. One of her probably had. Grace Macbloodycarthy, so eager to know where I'd be today, who was going to ring and leave a message for me. Who almost certainly had, on the tape that Peter had wiped. And in that message, casually, she'd have given me the information I needed.

The whole thing was a set-up. Why they were doing it, I still didn't know, or who besides Elspeth and Grace were involved. But they were drip-feeding me information, to keep me on my toes, to keep me interested. The whole thing was some kind of Oxford, Lewis Carroll joke.

That was only mildly irritating. I was being paid. But now they'd miscalculated, and it had gone wrong, and as far as I could see there wasn't a Plan B. Unless the ceiling would only be smashed if I was there; unless they'd wait for me to get there before playing whatever prank it was.

I couldn't count on it, though. I'd have to be Plan B, all by myself, in case people got hurt.

THEY DID NOT ACKNOWLEDGE ME THEN, the note said. It didn't narrow it down for me. If the Womun was Elspeth, as far as I knew she was unacknowledged everywhere. Even supposing Grace wasn't involved, she'd know how Elspeth thought, what she was likely to be referring to. But she was on her way to a literary festival in the West Country. So she'd said.

I wouldn't hang from her word at twenty thousand feet, but she was the most quick-witted of them, and the most practical. I didn't think she'd want casualties. I could call her place, and see if she'd left a number.

Failing her, Melanie might help.

I needed a phone.

Barty might have his mobile with him. Alan certainly would.

And both of them would probably be in Quaglino's by now. I hadn't seen them go in, but during the last few minutes Saddam Hussein could have gone in with Hillary Roddam Clinton on his arm for all I'd have noticed.

So I went in.

The girl at the reception and cloakroom desk, French, thirtyish, elegant in black and white, greeted me politely. 'The Prozzeroe table? Oh, so sorry, that booking was cancelled yestairday. Are you Alex Tannair?'

I was.

'I have a messahge for you.' She took a slip of paper from the reservations book, and passed it across to me. *Nice try*, it said.

If Barty'd been there I'd have slapped him. This was no time for jokey messahges. This was no time for anything, except a mobile.

I looked across at the tables in the bar, spotted a man with a mobile beside his drink, and went over to him. He was with another man; both fortyish, trendyish, in polo-necks and linen trousers and loose Italian jackets, both flushed enough to have been in the bar some time. I sat down on the extra chair at their table, leant forward to give them the benefit of the scoop neck in case they weren't gay, babbled something about being very grateful and it being very urgent, picked up the phone, flicked through my organizer, and dialled Grace.

I cut off as soon as the answering-machine

message clicked on.

I dialled Melanie. Three rings. Another answering machine.

Now what? Who? Melanie at the newspaper she wrote the column for. Tried it. She wasn't there.

I looked at my watch. One-sixteen.

'Can I get you a drink, at all?' said the owner of the phone. He had a round face, blond hair in a beautiful haircut, and smart glasses. He seemed entertained rather than annoyed, which was just as well. His friend had less hair, had spent less on his haircut, and showed no emotion.

'No thanks,' I said. Who was left? Janet Wilson was out. She hadn't even remembered Elspeth's name accurately. Unless she'd been putting it on. And getting any information out of Janet, even supposing she knew it, would take much too long.

'Oh, do have a drink,' said Cool Haircut. 'I insist.'

'Mineral water, please,' I said. I groped in my bag for the letter and read it again. *THEY DID NOT ACKNOWLEDGE ME THEN.* That first night I'd met her, she talked about the disappointing reception of her book. And about her lack of advancement at work.

The book angle was hopeless. Reviewers? Readers? It didn't point to a place. But the work just might. Who'd know where Elspeth had worked?

'Sparkling or still? Ice and lemon?' said Cool Haircut. His friend giggled.

'Still, please, ice, no lemon,' I said, and looked

233

at my watch again.

One-seventeen.

I didn't know anyone else who knew her. Or who might, by the wildest stretch of the imagination, know anything about her.

Yes I did. Barty.

I smiled at Cool Haircut. 'This really is very urgent,' I said as I dialled, and gave what I hoped was a seductive smile. The first I've ever tried. Pity I didn't see his reaction, because Jacqui answered straight away. 'Jacqui? This is Alex . . . Yes, hi . . . Listen, Jacqui, this is VERY IMPORTANT.'

Jacqui giggled. 'He said you'd say that,' she said.

'Who?'

'Who what?'

'Who said I'd say that?'

'Barty, of course. He told me all about the game you were playing. And it was very mean of you to trick me yesterday. And I know where he and Alan are having lunch, but you're not going to trick me again. So there. I'm going to ring off now.'

'Jacqui, wait —'

I was left holding a dead line.

I groaned. 'Do have some water,' said Cool Haircut. 'I ordered Evian; is that right?'

'Perfect,' I said, and gulped some, to shut him up while I thought.

I looked at my watch. One-eighteen.

I needed an angle of approach that would grab Jacqui straight away.

Soap-opera. I scraped together my memories of the nightmare month I'd worked as floor manager on *Love is the Answer*, then I dialled again.

'Jacqui, don't ring off — Jacqui, I want to tell you a secret. I'M HAVING HIS BABY!'

I must have spoken louder than I realized, because I stopped a waiter in his tracks, and conversation died at the nearby tables. But Jacqui didn't ring off. She whispered, in her little voice, 'Oh, Alex, I'm so happy for you! If it was planned, I mean?'

'Yes, oh yes,' I said. 'We've been secretly married for months.' The more ridiculous guff I gave her the more overwhelmed she'd be.

'Congratulations,' she said.

'Congratulations,' said Cool Haircut. His friend giggled again.

'I haven't told anybody but you. About the marriage. You won't tell anyone, will you?'

'Oh, no.'

'And I haven't even told Barty about the baby. And I want to, but we've had a stupid fight.'

'What about?'

My stock of clichéd invention was running out. I scraped the barrel. 'We've had a misunderstanding. He — he was jealous. He thought I was seeing another man.'

'But you weren't, were you?' she said anxiously.

'Oh, no. It was . . . it was the gynaecologist.' I had momentary doubts about whether she'd handle the word, but I'd underestimated her.

'Oh, poor you!'

'And I must see Barty, I must talk to him. If I don't, the gynaecologist says I could miscarry. From the stress. I must speak to him today. Now. I MUSTN'T LOSE OUR BABY!'

I took a deep breath and a sip of water. Cool Haircut patted my hand.

'Of course not,' said Jacqui. 'Of course not, Alex. They're at Daphne's.'

'Is Alan on the mobile?'

'Oh, yes. I have to ring him at one-thirty.'

'Can I have his number? Do you have it in front of you?' I asked cautiously.

'Yes.'

I grabbed my organizer and scribbled the number, while Cool Haircut held the phone to my ear. 'Thanks, Jacqui. You're a mate —'

I rang off. I felt mean. I rationalized it: this was important. But all the same I hadn't just been scraping the barrel, I'd been shooting a dim, sweetnatured fish in it.

'Are you all right, my dear?' said Cool Haircut. He looked half concerned, half unconvinced, as well he might.

One-twenty. Dial. Ring.

'Alan Protheroe,' said Alan, loudly.

'Alan, this is Alex. Don't hang up. I need to speak to Barty. Urgently. This isn't part of our game. This is WORK. This is MONEY.'

Two key words, for Alan, foolish as he was. He wouldn't have survived so long as an inde-

236

pendent producer if they hadn't been.

He covered the mouthpiece and I heard him mumbling to Barty.

'Sorry, Alex. Barty doesn't want to speak to you.'

'Alan, hold the phone so Barty can hear me.'

'Really, Alex . . .' Alan began.

'JUST DO IT!' I shouted.

'Very well,' he huffed, and then I could hear background noise.

'BARTY, I'M NOT KIDDING! BARTY! PLEASE! THIS IS URGENT!'

Pause.

Barty's voice. 'Alex?'

'We'll discuss us another time, OK? I need your help. I'm working on a case involving Grace Macarthy and the other Vestal Virgins. Do you know who I mean?'

'Melanie and Elspeth,' he said promptly.

'OK. After Elspeth left Oxford, where did she work for years? Where they didn't acknowledge her, before she left in a huff for the country?'

Pause. He didn't know, I thought, down to earth with a bump. Wishful thinking to suppose he would.

'The British Museum,' he said.

Chapter 25

The British Museum. A vast, straggling building, repository of perhaps the chief distinction and dignity the British still possessed, full of innocent tourists and school parties and lovers and scholars and — and glass ceilings. But one particular one: the Reading Room ceiling. Where people studied books Elspeth hadn't written, supplied by the institution that hadn't recognized her.

I looked at my watch. 1:21. I took a deep breath, and thought. The phone line hummed between us: Barty was waiting. 'Barty, I need you to clear the Museum, especially the round Reading Room. Bomb scare.' No time to explain about ceilings.

Pause. 'How long do I have?'

'Nine minutes.'

'Sure?' he said.

Now wasn't the time for doubts. 'Dead sure,' I said.

He hesitated for only about two seconds, but it seemed much longer. Then he said, 'Clear for one-thirty. You'd better be right, smartass,' and rang off.

Cool Haircut was appalled. 'I say —' he began.

'All under control. I'm Alex Tanner, Anti-Terrorist Squad,' I said, moving easily from one television genre to another. 'Your country thanks you.'

I thrust the mobile into his hands. 'Will my country pay for the calls?' he asked, recovering.

'Submit Form TR82B. In triplicate,' I said, and headed for the door. I had a mile to run. In eight minutes.

It's not easy to move quickly, dolled up. As I ran up Piccadilly to the Circus, the earrings slapping me with each stride, my tits bouncing, my patent leather flatties giving me only half-purchase on the pavements, I thought longingly of trainers and strong plain bras and sweatshirts and jeans. 99.9 per cent of the time, I could have done this on my head. Sod's Law. Some feminists hold that women sacrifice too much in making themselves attractive to men. 'Sisters, I'm with you,' I said out loud, dodging through the Circus traffic and accelerating up Shaftesbury Avenue, keeping to the gutters because they were clear of the aimless wandering sightseers I kept knocking into.

It was about a mile to the Museum. It could have been less. If Barty hadn't managed to clear the place I could barrel straight into the Reading Room and make enough of a fuss to clear that, at least.

I had a British Library Reader's ticket in the card-case in my bag. I'd dip for it when I reached Charing Cross Road; I didn't want to break my rhythm until I had to, for traffic. I was making good time, considering, and I accelerated for the last hundred yards to compensate for the time I'd lose in crossing the road.

I wove through the queues of cars, groping in the bottom of my bag. Card-case, crammed full. I collect memberships and credit cards: they make me feel important.

I was across Charing Cross Road, in the next section of Shaftesbury Avenue. I looked down at the cards in their little plastic folders. Flip video club, flip flip libraries, flip American Express, flip Visa, flip MOD.

MOD? Ministry of Defence? I had to force myself not to drop my speed. Of course. I'd worked on a Germ Warfare doco and spent a day at a Top Secret Establishment. I'd had to wear an identity card on my lapel. And I'd kept it.

MOD, it said, with my photograph. If you looked at the small print it was useless. But I wouldn't give anyone a chance to.

Yee-hah! I thought, running faster than I ever had in my life before.

I'd been going for over five minutes now. What was the police response-time likely to be? Unless Barty'd gone straight for the Museum authorities. No, I could trust Barty. The Museum was such an obvious terrorist target that there must be a police incident procedure in place for it. And Barty knew how the IRA worked. He knew the police number they called to give bomb warnings, and the code words they used to show it was a genuine threat.

New Oxford Street. I went straight over, hoping

to hell that there were no provincials at the wheel in the stream of steady traffic.

There weren't. Brakes screamed and irascible, quick-reacting London drivers shouted and swore at me and I waved as I accelerated up Bloomsbury Street and realized that I hadn't even mentioned to Barty that I expected him to use his IRA information to get the job done, that I just assumed he would.

He had. He must have done. I turned into Great Russell Street and after a few strides I could see into the forecourt of the Museum behind the great black iron railings, and it was full of people. Full. Marshalled in groups by uniformed Museum staff.

Barty, I love you, I thought as I slowed down, leant against the wall and gasped for breath. I checked my watch: 1:28. I'd done a six-minute mile, or thereabouts.

And now I wanted to get inside and save the ceiling. I loved the Reading Room; God knew what it would cost to replace that ceiling. If the country could or would afford it.

I heaved myself up and jogged between the crowds of people towards the wide shallow steps up to the front door. There were some uniformed police among the crowd and, I could hear from the screaming sirens, many more on their way, but none actually at the entrance. People were still hurrying out and I pushed myself in, against the crowd, flashing my MOD card at anyone who tried to stop me.

In the middle of the great hall, near the gift

shop, stood a group of people obviously directing operations. Several of them looked like senior plain-clothes police. Damn. My MOD card wouldn't wash with them, and police are trained to take things slowly and methodically. I skirted them cautiously and sidled up to the corridor leading to the Library entrance. A few Readers were still trickling out, women with straight hair and long drab skirts and big drab sweaters, men in dark suits or corduroy trousers and tweed jackets, looking mildly annoyed rather than alarmed.

There must still be Library staff in there, I thought. They'd have to stay to clear it like the captain of a ship.

I went in and looked up. The ceiling was intact, as I remembered it, a soaring cupola of lozenged glass cupping the pale blue and gold plasterwork of the lower walls. It must be eighty feet up, I thought. If that glass went it'd have killed someone. Maybe several people.

I looked round the desks, padded with blue leather or leather-look plastic, arranged in rows like the spokes of a wheel radiating from the area in the centre where the Library staff worked. The desks were empty, I saw, and then I was pounced on.

'Out! Out, please!' said the only remaining man in the room, obviously a librarian. He was middle-aged and middle-height and middle-bald, and he had his knickers in a major twist, and I didn't blame him. As far as he knew he and his precious

242

Library were going to be blown to hell and gone any second now.

'Alex Tanner, MOD,' I said, and flashed my card at him. 'We've had further information. The threat isn't a bomb threat, it's a specific threat to the ceiling.'

He looked up. I looked up. All either of us could see was grey London light filtering through an elegant pattern of semi-opaque white glass.

'If someone was going to smash that, how would they get up there? Can we stop them?'

'We need to tell the Museum,' he said agitatedly.

'Aren't you the Museum?'

'No. Of course not. I'm the Library,' he said. 'There's a walkway. And ladders. There's access for cleaning. You can go through the Snow Gallery, or Paints and Drawings — MNLA. Or the 1850s book stack, if you're Library.'

'Go and tell them,' I said. 'Anyone. Get anyone up there, now. I'll stay here.'

'But —'

'MOD,' I said. 'Priority. Do you want to save the ceiling or not?'

He went.

I looked at my watch. 1:30.

And then I looked up and saw them. Figures, through the glass. At least two, but the glass was too opaque to see at all clearly. I stepped back, almost to the wall, and prepared to cover my eyes; but I couldn't not watch. I had to see.

Smash! One of the twenty segments had gone,

243

and the shards of glass sprayed out and down. I watched them fall. It was the section farthest from me; I was safe enough, though the thuds as the larger pieces sliced into the desks made me shudder.

I looked up again. I could half see through the gap, two figures struggling. They looked male. One had a weapon — an axe? An ice-axe? I couldn't see.

Smash! Another section had gone, and one of the figures was slumped, awkwardly, over the gap. It was wide enough to slip through. If he was unconscious, he probably would.

He looked unconscious. He looked familiar.

It was Teddy.

He was bleeding, badly. I watched blood stain some of the shattered pieces still clinging to the metal struts (iron?) that reinforced the ceiling, and start to drip over and down into the Reading Room.

'Hold on!' I shouted, as his weight started to shift. 'Hold on!' and I turned to run for help.

As I turned, he slipped through the metal bars. His body seemed to float down, relaxed, riding the air like a stuntman doing a dead fall.

He landed on his front across two desks, and I tried not to hear the noise as he landed, so I wouldn't have to remember it, though I knew I would.

I ran over to him. He was obviously dead. The upright of the desks had snapped his spine, and a side of his face was smashed in.

I tried Emergency Aid anyway, even though the emergenry was well past. I cleared his airway — I think a part of the bloody debris my fingers hooked out was splinters of bone from his face — and I gave him mouth-to-mouth resuscitation until someone pulled me away.

They took me into an office. They talked at me as we went. I gathered that, officially, I was in deep trouble for impersonating an employee of the Ministry of Defence.

Unofficially, the trouble went deeper. My fingers could still remember the boyish smoothness of the skin of his shattered face, and the patch of strong stubble he'd missed with the razor that morning, when he felt proud of himself for whatever he'd discovered that he thought would help me, when he thought that he was going to talk to me at eight-thirty and tell me all about it, and I'd be pleased.

They were embarrassed when I started to cry. It wasn't their fault they weren't being rough with me. Actually I think they were trying to be understanding, as far as official understanding ever goes. They couldn't know why I was crying. I wasn't sure myself; though when they called it shock that made them feel better.

Saturday, 2 October

Chapter 26

I slept in, next morning. It was gone ten by the time I dragged myself downstairs and addressed myself to the task of making coffee.

Coffee-making was about as complicated a task as I was up to. It was almost beyond me. I felt dead-legged and woollen-headed and as I finally gripped the mug and sipped and looked through the kitchen window at the bright clear sun outside, I seriously considered going back to bed for the day.

The authorities had finally let me go latish the previous night. The Anti-Terrorist Squad had given up first. No IRA involvement, they muttered, sounding disappointed, and left me to the Special Branch.

The Special Branch were slower on the uptake, or more thorough, or better manned. They kept at me for longer. Then, disappointed, they'd handed me over to the Ministry of Defence, who seemed excited by the prospect that anyone should want to impersonate them, and reluctant to drop me until they'd fully explored my motives. They finally, grudgingly, told me they weren't going to press charges, and glided away.

Then I was moved to a police station and the coppers had their turn. They hung on to me longest of all, since Teddy's death was their business. I told them everything I knew about Elspeth. I suggested that Edward Webb was involved. I still didn't know, myself, who the other figure on the ceiling at the Museum had been. It could have been Elspeth; it could have been Edward; it could even have been Grace, although I didn't think so, and I didn't suggest her to them.

The police kept asking me if Teddy's death was accidental. I didn't know. I just described it to them, again and again, and felt worse about it each time.

It wasn't until I'd been with the police for hours that I began to wonder why they hadn't caught the other person, or people, involved at the Museum. I asked them. They muttered about delay and confusion and public safety, and I realized through my apathy that they'd probably been so busy worrying about my impersonation that the librarian hadn't managed to persuade them to get anybody up to the ceiling in time.

Eventually the police drove me home and I gave them the Womun's letters and envelopes for evidence, and the tape with her first call. Peter was there, and he looked after me. When I'd had a bath and gone to bed, he went to rescue Polly's Golf, which would have been clamped or towed away long since.

I'd fallen asleep before he got back so I didn't know if he'd managed to find the car, I realized, and poured myself more coffee. Life was coming back to my brain. Slowly.

I wondered what Melanie felt. Poor Melanie. And whether Grace had heard. And what Elspeth was doing, and if the police had found her.

My brief interest slipped away. I didn't want to think about it.

I went into the living-room to lie on the sofa. The answering-machine light was flashing. Several messages, apparently. And a note: *9.30 A.M. Saturday. Have to go out, back about late afternoon — Golf parked outside, keys on hook in kitchen — Barty O'Neill rang, is coming round eleven o'clock — other messages on machine, nothing vital. Take good care, love Peter.*

I should have been relieved to get the car back. I should have felt something about Barty. I just went to lie on the sofa and closed my eyes, and tried to think of something that wasn't Teddy.

I must have fallen asleep because when the doorbell rang and I blinked at the video clock it was 11.07. I dragged through to the kitchen, opened the window, and whistled at the top of Barty's head. 'Keys coming down,' I called, and chucked them.

I was back on the sofa when he came in, my eyes closed.

'Hi,' he said.

'Hi,' I said.

'You look terrible,' he said gently.

'I looked great yesterday,' I said defensively. 'I borrowed Polly's green linen Armani jacket, and nobody looked at me oddly in Quaglino's.'

'Did you want them to?'

'No, that's the point. Ordinarily, they would have stared. Because I'm not the Quaglino's type.' I opened my eyes and looked at him. He'd sat down in the armchair opposite. He was wearing old brown corduroy trousers, a dark blue shirt and a once-expensive, now battered, brown knitted silk sweater. He didn't look like the Quaglino's type either. He just looked like Barty, and I was so glad to see him that for a dreadful moment I thought I was going to cry again.

'You're completely wrong,' he said.

I never, never fail to rise to that. 'I'm wrong?' I snapped, sitting up. 'What about?'

'About nobody staring at you in Quaglino's. According to my source, you announced our secret marriage and the imminent arrival of our baby to an enthralled audience of pre-lunch drinkers.'

'Oh shit,' I said. Then I started to laugh. I couldn't not. 'Who's your source?'

'I never —' He began the first and only media commandment.

'— reveal my sources,' we both chanted together.

'Do you mind?' I said.

'What about?'

'About — about the baby.'

'Not at all, though I have for some time hoped to play a part, however small, in its conception,' he said primly.

I tried not to laugh. 'Jacqui's just such a soap-

252

opera birdwit,' I said. 'It was all I could think of.'

'Don't apologize. It was very well played,' he said lightly.

'Thanks for calling the police.'

'Not at all.'

'Who did you say you were?'

'Semtex Sean.'

'That's awful! You didn't!' I said, trying to look disapproving, and collapsing into laughter.

'That's better,' he said.

'You're trying to cheer me up,' I said accusingly. I hate being manipulated.

'I'm not,' he said. 'I'm succeeding.'

The bang of the front door and footsteps on the stairs saved me from having to agree. Barty was frowning. 'Barstow promised he'd stay out of the way,' he said.

The scratch of the key in the lock was followed by Nick. I introduced them. Nick nearly smiled at us both and wolf-whistled at me. 'The program's running,' she said. 'He doesn't need me till Monday. Can I have a bath?'

'Sure,' I said, and she went upstairs.

I explained who she was, briefly. Barty looked unsurprised. Then I told him about Kinross, his obsession, our deal and Nick's help, and he looked even less surprised. 'He might crack it, at that,' he said. 'Did you get the information you wanted?'

'I did, but I haven't even looked at it. I haven't had time.'

'Are you too upset to tell me what's been going on?' he said.

I was piqued. 'Too upset? Me?' I swung my legs over the side of the sofa and sat up. It was only then I realized that I was naked.

They must have been right. I *was* in shock. I'd had clues: the roughness of the sofa material against my flesh; Nick's wolf-whistle. But I hadn't picked them up. I'd been naked the whole time; I hadn't known, and Barty — Barty'd said I looked terrible.

I pulled myself together. I wasn't going to let him know I hadn't known. So I was a naturist, so what?

'Why don't you go and put something on?' he said mischievously.

He knew.

'No thanks, I'm fine,' I said. I had to butch it out. I arranged my limbs in as near an approximation as I could manage to the position of Goya's *Naked Maja*, and I told him about the Womun in the Balaclava Helmet.

Then I went upstairs.

Then I blushed.

Chapter 27

I had to wait till Nick was out of the bath to shower, and by then the hot water was tepid. I didn't mind: I showered in cold. I needed to wake up. As the shock wore off, I began to feel involved again. It hadn't, as far as I could see, been my fault that Teddy had died, but neither had I done what the Womun had paid me to do: I hadn't stopped her.

I still owed her that duty, or some duty. She was my client, however half-baked. Or murderous.

After the shower, I cleaned my teeth, dressed, and went downstairs. Barty and Nick were in the kitchen. She was scrambling eggs, he was watching her, leaning against my noticeboard. He was too tall for my kitchen. The ceiling wasn't eight feet at its highest point, sloping down as it neared the window (was something wrong with the bedroom floor above?) and it cleared his head by only inches.

I'd have to change my man, I thought flippantly. Or my flat.

Then I realized what I'd thought. Change the flat? Never. Never. Silently, I apologized to my flat.

Nick looked up. 'I'm making scrambled eggs on toast for all of us. That's all that's in the fridge, and that's all I can cook anyway, without recipe books. You don't have any recipe books.'

'Get a move on, then,' I said. 'We've got work to do.'

Barty pushed himself away from the wall. 'D'you want me to go?'

'No,' I said, rather hurt. 'D'you want to?'

'If you want to work, I mean,' he said.

'You're going to help.'

'Have you a fee structure in mind?'

'Yes. A share of Nick's scrambled eggs and the satisfaction of a job well done. A fair offer.'

'I'll remember that you think it a fair offer next time I hire you,' he said.

'Eggs are ready,' said Nick.

As soon as we'd eaten I told Barty what I wanted him to do and left him in the sitting-room with the phone. Nick and I were in the kitchen, going through Kinross's file on Edward Webb. I explained what we were looking for — any reference to the Vestal Virgins, particularly in their last term at Oxford — and then divided the material up. I still didn't trust myself to fire on all cylinders so I deliberately gave her the most promising stuff, and more than half of the total.

I finished first, with nothing productive. Mine had been notes on Webb's graduate supervisions: more or less solid maths. Then I just sat and watched her read, and tried not to think about Teddy. Finally she looked up. 'That's it,' she said.

'So what happened in the Finals term of 1971?'
I said.

'It was a big mess. At the beginning of term
St Scholastica's were flipping their lid because
Grace was obviously pregnant, and she named
Edward as the father.'

'*Grace* was? Fennel is Edward's child?'

'That's what it says here. This Janet Wilson
woman got on to Balliol, and then Edward asked
permission to marry Grace —'

'He asked permission? How old was he?'

'That's not the point. It was a college rule —
undergraduates weren't allowed to marry, and if
he broke college rules he couldn't sit his exams.
He asked permission and he was granted it by
the Master, against Kinross's advice. Kinross
thought it would ruin his career. But after all
that, Grace wouldn't marry him.'

'Why not?'

'She said she didn't want to, apparently. She
said no one had consulted her, and she'd arrange
her own life, thank you. So it went quiet for a
bit, though Edward was gated for a week or two,
I suppose to remind him not to want to marry
women who didn't want to marry him, or for
wasting the Master's time, or for having sex with
a member of the University, or something. Then
Elspeth did her nut. She started bleeding in the
middle of the night in College and woke everybody up and the college doctor was called and
said she'd had a botched backstreet abortion, and
she was taken to the Radcliffe Infirmary, where

they saved the baby.'

'They *saved* the baby?'

'And then she said Edward was the father, and that he'd arranged the abortion.'

'While still gated?'

'It's not funny,' she said, bewildered.

'Sorry,' I said, trying to sober up. It was serious, of course it was, but it was a long time ago, and struck me as farcical.

Nick went on, ignoring me. 'So Janet Wilson wrote to Kinross and said Edward Webb would have to marry Elspeth. It was what Elspeth wanted. So the Master gave permission. Then Edward Webb said he wouldn't, and Elspeth cracked up.'

'How?'

'Nervous breakdown. She was moved straight from the Radcliffe Infirmary to the Warneford — that must have been the local mental hospital. That was three weeks before her exams. And a week later, she was smuggled out of the Warneford and taken up to London, where she had another abortion. Successful this time. And she went back in to the Warneford and cracked up completely, and told them who had arranged the abortion and taken her up to London, et cetera.'

'And that was Edward?'

'Not just Edward. Edward, and Melanie Slater.'

'*Babykiller,*' I said. 'Of course. That's what Elspeth wrote on Melanie's wall, when she broke in last Sunday.' I was beginning to feel for her. She'd been everybody's pawn.

'So then Edward was in deep trouble. The Master wanted to send him down for bringing the college into disrepute, but Kinross spoke up for him. He obviously didn't like him — you should read some of his comments — but he thought he was a real mathematician. So Edward was rusticated — that seems to be what they call suspended — but allowed to come back to sit his exams. And when he'd sat the exams and got his results and been accepted to do his graduate degree, he married.'

'Who?'

'Melanie Slater.'

I whistled. 'So Melanie's still married to him? And living in sin with her smart mock-husband? And little Bella is a bastard?'

Nick was right, it was a mess. A major mess. Poor Elspeth. By a stupid accident of biology, she'd been torn apart.

Then I rethought it. She needn't have got pregnant in the first place. And if she had, she should have taken care of herself. Or could she? The little pointy-faced creature in the punt photograph didn't look as if she could take care of a stuffed toy.

'Just a minute,' said Nick. 'Is this Edward Webb character still alive? I thought you said Teddy wanted you to find his father, but that you thought he was probably dead.'

I'd forgotten how long ago it had been since I'd briefed Nick. I was just about to explain when she said, 'Teddy will be pleased, won't he? That's good. I like Teddy.'

It wasn't her fault, but when she said that, I saw him fall, again. I heard him land. And I tried to breathe into his shattered face.

'What's the matter, Alex?' she said. 'What is it?'

I heard Barty coming into the kitchen, but I couldn't see him, because the room was going round. Then I felt his hand on my forehead, and something in front of me, under my chin.

'Barty?' I said.

'Yes. Barty with basin,' he said.

Chapter 28

While I was being sick, I could half hear Barty explaining to Nick what had happened at the British Library yesterday. It saved me doing it, anyway.

After that I sipped water for a while, then I went up to clean my teeth, wobbly-legged and frustrated. This wasn't like me. I'm usually tough. Much worse things have happened to me without having this effect. It was terrible about Teddy, of course it was, but me cracking under it wasn't helping anyone; certainly not him. He was beyond help, and I firmly believe that if people are beyond help you shouldn't waste energy worrying about them.

Perhaps it was just that I'd seen him die. Or that he hadn't deserved it. Or that he was so young. Or that he'd liked my breasts.

I sat on the edge of the bath with a wet face-cloth on the back of my neck, and tried to get a grip. On anything.

When I felt less dizzy I went down again. They'd moved into the living-room. Nick looked scared; I couldn't imagine why. But I didn't want her to, and if she was scared because of me, I had to reassure her.

I didn't trust my voice, and I was right, because

it came out high and quavery when I said, 'I'm fine. Really.'

Barty looked at me. 'Good,' he said. 'I spoke to my police contact. They haven't found Elspeth yet. Or Edward. The dogs are being looked after by a neighbour. Elspeth arranged that yesterday morning. She said she wouldn't be back till Monday.'

With every word he spoke I felt stronger. 'Did you get Grace?' I asked.

'I know where she is. I spoke to Fennel, and she gave me Grace's number at the hotel, and the number of the Festival office. I was just going to ring them when I came into the kitchen.'

'To give me your Florence Nightingale,' I said.

'Exactly so, though perhaps not so much the Lady with the Lamp as the Man with the Basin. One of my best.'

'Thanks,' I said.

'Not at all. The least I could do, after you gave me your Botticelli's Venus earlier . . . Shall I try the Festival now?'

'You — you treacherous *snake*,' I said. 'I'm not in the least like Botticelli's Venus. And it wasn't like that.'

'Wasn't like what?'

'I've taken up naturism,' I said. 'A healthy hobby.'

Nick was watching us, her head moving back and forth like a Centre Court audience at Wimbledon. 'Alex, are you all right? Really?' she said.

'Yes, I am,' I said, and I nearly was. 'Ring the Festival, Barty.'

It took a while to get Grace, and when she came on the line Barty passed her over to me without speaking. Lucky, because I was beginning to feel the stirrings of jealousy again, with him actually in front of me. Was it lucky, or was it diplomatic? He made the Cresta Run look like a cheese-grater.

'Alex?' said Grace. 'What happened?' For the first time since I'd known her, she wasn't chuckling. Even if you couldn't quite hear it, the chuckle was usually there, like the murmur of an underground river. Now it had gone, and she sounded older. And more New Zealand.

'Did you hear about Teddy?'

'Yes. It was on last night's news . . . It's dreadful. Didn't you get my message?'

'No. The tape was damaged,' I said. 'Someone spilt coffee on it.'

'Well,' she said, and fell silent. At least she wasn't a drag-it-out person, a just-fancy-that person.

'Do you think it was an accident?' I said.

'Of course it was. Teddy wasn't supposed to be there. He knew nothing about it. Any of it. Though he started it off, in a way.'

'How?'

'When he told Elspeth that you were a private detective. And a television researcher. After he saw your advertisement in the post office. He knew she liked women who did audacious things.'

I felt far from audacious. I felt, irrationally, responsible. 'So how did that start Elspeth off?'

'I don't know, exactly,' she said. Not a form of words, I suspected, that she often had occasion to use.

'Guess,' I said.

'Partly that she was upset by Leona's death . . . and I said, to cheer her up, that death helps a writer — any artist — because of the publicity. And she thought she'd get publicity for all of us if she set up the Womun stunt, and she thought that if she hired you, with all your media contacts, you'd help. Unknowingly, of course.'

No wonder I'd felt manipulated. 'Didn't she mind who she hurt, with the ceiling?'

'She wasn't going to smash it. Just splash paint on it, and upset everyone, and leave a note from the Womun.'

'And you went along with all this?'

There was a silence. Then she said, 'You know how it is, with old friends. Sometimes you love them more than you agree with them. More than you enjoy their company. More than you have in common, after a while. Elspeth was hard work.'

'So to escape her emotional demands, you went along with her?'

'Yes. I didn't think it would do any harm. And it wouldn't have. Elspeth's safe. She's very conventional. She wouldn't have smashed that ceiling, however much she hated the Museum lot. It was Edward, it must have been. It worried me when you said he was involved. I got on to Elspeth straight away, to warn her to keep him out of it, but she said she could handle him. She said he was enjoying himself, and he got little enough fun, and she was going to take him along. She was proud of her plan. She wanted company, I think.'

'But how did Teddy get involved?'

'I've no idea. No idea at all.'

Perhaps his telephone message would have told me, I thought.

Grace was speaking again. 'How is Elspeth? Have they locked Edward up?'

'They haven't found her,' I said. 'They haven't found either of them. Where will they have gone?'

Silence.

'If you know, you must tell the police,' I said. 'And get them a good lawyer.'

'I don't know,' she said.

I covered the mouthpiece of the receiver. 'Barty, get her to tell you where they're likely to be. Elspeth's still my client. She needs looking after. So does he, by all accounts.'

Barty looked cautious. I suppose he was trying to estimate how much I knew about his relationship with Grace, and how jealous I was likely to be. 'Why me?' he said.

'Because you were her lover,' I said. 'Because she still fancies you. Because you've known her for twenty-four years and I met her last Tuesday, all right? Come on, Nick, we'll leave him to it.'

It didn't take him long, and I didn't listen, not to a single word. I despise women who want to take a man and wipe out every single relationship he's ever had right up to the moment he first looked into their short-sighted eyes. I wasn't going to be one of them, if I could help it. Never. Though I was, I feared, by nature. Or perhaps by circumstance.

Grace needed help. I didn't want to imagine how bad she must feel about the tragic mess she'd partly created, or at least had failed to prevent. Barty'd be a good person for her to talk to. So I didn't think about what they were saying or how pleased he might be feeling to hear her voice or about any of the past they shared, but concentrated on clearing the action board.

The action list went first. I wrote another, with just one item:

Arabella Trigg — report

I took down the text of the *Guardian* article and binned it. Then I reached for the photograph, which of course Barty had taken. That was Barty's framing and Barty's eye; Grace had all but named him to me, in the bath, and I hadn't listened. I wondered as I crumpled it up which of the Vestal Virgins had spent the night with him after that day on the river back in 1969. When I'd been five.

'Are you all right, Alex?' said Nick.

266

'Yes. Why, does it worry you if I'm not?' I said.

'Because you're so indestructible, usually, I suppose.'

'Nobody's indestructible,' I said, 'and you've only known me five days, and any investigator who wasn't upset by the violent death of a perfectly healthy, intelligent, interesting young client would be a nutter, don't you think? Specially if it happened right in front of their eyes.'

'Would you like a coffee?' she said.

'Definitely,' I said.

She was learning.

Chapter 29

It was twenty past six, just after sunset. The darkening sky was washed with delicate pink, and the air smelt of dying summer. Barty's BMW was parked in a layby two hundred yards from Grace's Oxfordshire cottage, and Barty and I were sitting in the front, waiting. Nick was in the back. She hadn't wanted to be left out, and with that number of people, another couldn't hurt. We were waiting for the other cars.

Several of them. Grace was sure that Elspeth and Edward would have holed up in her cottage, but she was prepared for Barty to tell me that only if I agreed to let her make her own arrangements about who else was there.

She wanted time to drive up from the West Country herself. She wanted a lawyer. And she wanted to invite Melanie Slater.

Barty'd agreed on my behalf. When he told me, I just nodded. If Grace wanted a circus, then she could have it, so long as I managed to get hold of Elspeth and sort her out.

A large Audi was the first car to draw up behind us. Inside, Melanie Slater and a man I recognized from her drawing-room photographs as her husband, Nigel Meades. I was surprised she'd been prepared to come.

Barty went to talk to them. When he came back, I said, 'How is she?'

He shrugged. 'As you'd expect. Very — sad.'

'Not angry?'

'Who with?'

'Elspeth? Edward? Grace? Me?'

'No. She doesn't seem to be. Nigel's angry, though.'

'Why?'

'They were supposed to be going to an important dinner-party tonight. Important to him.'

'Melanie wouldn't have gone to that anyway,' I said. 'The night after Teddy died?'

'No, but Nigel would.'

'So why didn't he go, and let Melanie come here by herself? Or did he think she wasn't up to it?'

'No,' he said. 'He's jealous of Grace.'

'How, jealous? Sexually?'

'No. Territorially.'

Barty knew them too well. All of them. I shifted my body further down the seat and wedged my feet up on the glove compartment in front of me. It might scratch his precious car, but I didn't care.

Barty looked at me and smiled, and I nearly moved my feet. He'd seen through me before I had. I hate that.

I had to say something. 'Barty, why didn't Melanie tell Teddy his father was alive? Come to that, why didn't Grace?'

'It was Melanie's decision. She's always believed

if something isn't talked about, it isn't happening. She never accepted that Edward hadn't loved her enough. Plus Edward wanted to be dead. He didn't want to see Teddy. Perhaps, more importantly, he didn't want Teddy to see him, not as he was. After the accident.'

'And Fennel?'

'What about Fennel?'

'Didn't he see Fennel? She was his child, after all.'

'Grace never let Edward have anything to do with Fennel,' said Barty. Then he laughed. Rather admiringly, I thought. 'She said he was a competent lover but he'd be a lousy father.'

Another car. A classic sports car, a long, low, black Jaguar XK something or other. An expensive, eccentric, amazin', 'look-at-me' car. 'That'll be Grace's car,' I said as it parked behind the Audi. I couldn't see the driver.

Barty laughed.

The Jaguar driver got out and walked forward to the Audi. I watched her in the wing mirror. She was in her late thirties, with jaw-length blonde hair, strong features and a designer trouser-suit.

'Who the hell is this?' I said.

'The lawyer,' said Barty and Nick in chorus.

'Oh.'

'Don't tell me,' said Barty mischievously. 'You expected a man. Concentrate, Alex, you're with the sisterhood now.'

'I'm a sister,' I said defensively. I tried to be. When I remembered.

'Sharpen up, then, sister,' he said.

Then Grace arrived. In a battered three-year-old Volvo estate.

Grace wanted to go in first. The lawyer, Kate Fox, insisted on going with her. The rest of us followed in a cautious, straggling bunch. Melanie was grim-faced and silent and urban in her short-skirted suit and high heels. Nigel — a tallish, suited, well-kept, almost handsome man — was sulky.

The rest of us stood at the gate and watched Grace and Kate walk the ten yards up the paved path through the half-wild, September garden to the front door.

The cottage didn't look inhabited. The front was yellow stone covered with honeysuckle; the deep small windows were dark. It was twilight. There should have been lights on inside, I thought, if Elspeth and Edward were there.

We'd all come a long way, for nothing.

But when Grace reached the front door she bent to pick up a large stone and groped under it. Her hand came up empty. She gave a 'thumbs-up' sign and used the key on her car keyring.

Surely not even Grace would keep a key to her country cottage under a stone by the front door, I thought.

She opened the door and they both went in.

We waited.

Then they came out again, with Elspeth. She

271

was clutching something to her blocky chest, tightly.

We walked forward to the door and the sweet scent of honeysuckle.

Elspeth was crying. She only saw Melanie. She moved towards her and said, 'I'm so sorry. So, so sorry. Oh, Melanie, I'm so sorry.'

She opened her arms and Melanie went into them, and they clung together, and Melanie began to cry.

And then I saw that what Elspeth was holding in her right hand, behind Melanie's back, was a gun. A small hand-gun: a pistol.

I went to take it, but Barty held my arm, and I stopped.

Elspeth was talking. 'It was an accident, Melanie. Teddy just turned up at the Museum and waited at the entrance and followed us. He'd found out about the plan. He heard you talking to me on the phone. He heard Alex's name so he listened, he said. And he wanted to come along with his father and we had to do it on time otherwise we wouldn't have got away, and I really wanted to annoy them. I did. But if I'd known — oh, Melanie, if I'd known — I'd never have taken him with us, of course, but then we got up there and Edward was going to kill himself and jump through the ceiling, but I didn't know that, and Teddy tried to stop him, and then it happened. Edward didn't mean it. He hasn't spoken since . . . He won't speak to me. He wants to die, Melanie. He couldn't bear it, and neither can I. Teddy . . . My darling, darling Teddy . . .'

'Bloody nonsense,' said Nigel Meades. 'This is all childish, bloody nonsense.' He gripped Melanie by the shoulders and tugged her backwards. Elspeth clung on more tightly: Melanie didn't pull away from her.

Barty tapped Nigel on the back. 'Let her go,' he said.

Nigel turned on him. 'What's it to do with you?' he said.

'They're friends of mine,' said Barty. 'Old friends. And they're both upset.'

'And I don't know what to do with Edward,' said Elspeth. 'He was looking for Grace's gun, so I took it, and I kept it down my bra. He didn't know it was there. So then he went into the garage and he soaked himself with petrol, and he says he's going to set light to himself. But he doesn't have any matches, because I took those too. And then he fell asleep.'

'When was that, Elspeth?' said Grace.

'About an hour ago. He fell asleep, because we couldn't sleep last night, either of us. And I've been to look every five minutes or so. We should go and look again —'

'Melanie, I'm going home,' said Nigel. 'We should never have come. This is too much for you. The last thing you need is to be involved with that maniac.'

'He's not a maniac,' said Elspeth. 'He's ill, and you know it, Nigel.' She was stroking Melanie's back. 'Take the gun, Grace,' she said. 'It's getting in my way . . .'

Grace took the gun and vanished inside the cottage.

'We should go to Edward,' said Elspeth. 'Let's go to Edward.'

Melanie nodded and they started to walk round the side of the cottage, with Kate Fox in close attendance.

Grace emerged from the front door and followed them.

Nigel Meades cursed under his breath and followed Grace.

Barty, Nick and I followed him.

The garage was empty. Its doors were open and I could just see, through the dusk, Edward's body inside, propped against the back wall. His arms clasped his knees and his head was bent, but as we got nearer he raised his head and screamed.

There were no words: just a scream.

Everyone stopped.

In the quiet, I heard Melanie sobbing, and I could smell petrol.

Edward screamed again, and then subsided into a wail. It wasn't a child's, but it wasn't a thinking adult's either. It was the nearest a human being could get to a dog's bewildered whimper.

Even Nigel was silenced. Then Grace spoke. 'Edward,' she said. 'Hey, Edward, this is Grace.'

'Hello, Grace,' said Edward, almost normally. His voice was the true bass Teddy's would have been, if Teddy had had time. 'I want your gun.'

'Now look here —' Nigel began.

'Coming over,' said Grace, and lobbed it. It was a perfect under-arm lob: Edward had only to open his hands.

Melanie cried out and tried to move, but Elspeth held her.

'Kate,' said Grace, 'why don't you go and call the police?'

'I say —' said Nigel.

'I think I will,' said Kate, already ten feet away and accelerating, as Edward scrabbled in his pocket.

Barty had moved to a stand-pipe beside the garage and was putting a wide tub under it. I just heard the scrape of metal against metal as Edward loaded the pistol, before it was drowned by the thunder of water drumming into the tub.

Nick was just behind me, her sloe eyes fixed on Edward's hand, and the pistol. He lifted it to his temple and I turned to face her. 'Nick!' I said urgently, 'behind you!'

She spun round, only half taken-in, and as she moved I heard the shot, then a whoomph of igniting petrol vapour, then the splatter-splash of water.

By the time I looked into the garage again there was no fire. Edward's body was sodden. The light was almost gone: you couldn't tell blood from water. Both were pools of darkness beside his head.

Chapter 30

Grace herded us into the cottage and turned on some lamps. 'Drinks all round, I think,' she said. 'Barty?'

'Of course,' said Barty, and disappeared through a door on the left. I looked around the room. It was living-room and dining-room both, with low ceilings and an uneven stone floor and plenty of chintz chairs which had probably last had springs when they put out the 'UNSINKABLE' press release for the maiden voyage of the *Titanic*. It also had its share of Grace clutter, with slight country variations such as binding-twine and gro-bags.

Elspeth took Melanie up the stairs which led from a door beyond the fireplace. Nigel walked to the back of the room, past the dining-table, and stared resolutely through the french windows, his back to the room and his every muscle radiating disapproval. Kate and Grace were in conference by the telephone.

'Sit down, Nick,' I said. 'Are you OK?'

'Just about,' she said shakily. 'I've never — I'm glad I didn't see it.'

A normal kid, for once. 'So'm I,' I said, and perched on the arm of her chair.

Barty came in with champagne glasses on a

tray, full of a pink-tinted liquid, and handed them round. We all took one, except for Nigel. He said, 'What the hell is this?'

'Kir Royale, Nigel,' said Grace.

'Any chance of a decent malt?'

Barty went to a sideboard, took out a bottle, poured the drink and took it to him. 'Glenmorangie all right?' he said in the light voice he always used to cover his fury.

Grace chuckled. 'Say yes, Nigel, or you'll get the glass in your face.'

'We won't be here long,' he said ungraciously. 'This'll do.' He walked over to the stairs and shouted up, 'Melanie! We're going!'

She reappeared, with Elspeth behind her, and started to walk to the door, but then she subsided into a chair and said, 'I'd just like to sit down for a moment, Nigel, if you don't mind.'

Kate Fox said mildly, 'I must advise you that no one should leave before the police get here, Mr Meades.'

He looked about to explode.

'Elspeth,' I said loudly. 'I'd like to know why you did it. The whole thing.'

She looked at me blankly. 'Oh — of course, you don't know. Well. It was for the publicity, you see.'

She gave me her squirrel look; wilted, but would-be perky.

'For the publicity?'

'Yes. Of course. When Leona died her sales went up, and the same happened to Van Gogh.

And I didn't want to die, of course, but I thought death threats would be almost the same thing. And they'd re-publish my book, and people would read it. And it would help Grace and Melanie too, because they have books in the autumn list. And then it all went horribly wrong.' She started to cry.

'That was an accident,' said Grace firmly. 'A terrible accident.'

'But now they're both dead.'

Grace knelt beside her and took her hands. 'Drink up,' she said, holding a glass to her lips. 'Edward wanted to die. He should have died long ago. Teddy — Teddy is a tragedy. Nobody's fault.'

'I really thought, people should read my book. Women should. Because they need to know. They need to understand, about what keeps them down. The male conspiracy. I'm right, aren't I, Grace?'

'Hush,' said Grace, smoothing her hair. 'Not now.'

Nigel had gone back to his feet-apart landowner stance, looking out of the french windows. 'Male conspiracy, huh,' he said with contempt. 'There's no such thing. There doesn't need to be. You women can cock it up all by yourselves.'

Most of us — Kate, Grace, Nick and me — stared at him with varying degrees of contemptuous pity; a gesture wasted on his back. Elspeth looked at Grace. Melanie cried.

Then Grace said, more mildly than I expected, with one eye on Melanie, 'I see what you mean,

Nigel. We make mistakes.'

'Not just mistakes. Huge staggering bloody cock-ups, all the time, without us to help you.'

'Whereas you think men don't,' said Barty, lightly; 'responsible as they are for most of the non-natural disasters in recorded history?'

'That's because men *are* recorded history,' said Nigel, 'and I don't know whose side you think you're on, O'Neill.'

Then — fortunately — the police came.

When I woke up, it was half past eleven. I blinked at the large cheap garish Mickey Mouse alarm-clock on the bedside table, which was wearing a condom on each ear, and tried to work out where I was. Grace's bed, that was it. Grace's bed in Grace's cottage.

I'd given my statement early on, to a minor policeman. The major ones were concentrating on Elspeth and dealing chiefly with Kate Fox. Then I'd had another drink and fallen asleep in my chair, and Grace had taken me upstairs to her room.

I got out of bed and looked through the window. It was narrow and low; I had to bend my knees. It was a moonlit night, very still. The trees weren't moving. The garden was empty: the police must have gone. I looked over to the layby. All our cars were still there.

I went to the bathroom and splashed my face with water, and then went downstairs.

The dishevelled room had taken on a slightly

raffish air. Nigel was sitting alone at the dining-table wading his way through a plateful of chops and mashed potatoes, with a near-empty bottle of claret at his elbow. Grace, Kate, Elspeth, Melanie, Nick and Barty were sitting crosslegged in a circle. There were two joints on the go. John Lennon was singing 'Imagine'. Loudly.

I closed my eyes and opened them again. This was time-travel, surely? I'd gone to sleep in the nineties and woken up in the sixties.

But I'd also gone to sleep in a cottage bleak with grief and woken up to a party.

Another Grace Experience.

They moved over to make room for me and I sat down, between Grace and Barty. Such a suave pair.

I sucked at the joint and passed it on.

'We fooled you, didn't we?' said Elspeth, and she giggled.

'You did,' I agreed, trying not to sound too many joints behind. I had no idea what, specifically, she was talking about.

'We did,' said Melanie. 'We did. We fooled you.'

'You didn't expect me to kill my own dog, did you?' said Elspeth. 'Poor Gunny, but he was ill, and decapitation isn't painful, you know. Merciful, really. And he trusted me, so he wasn't afraid.'

'And you really thought I didn't want you to know about Mopsy,' said Melanie.

'It was supposed to be a mystery,' said Elspeth.

'So you'd be interested. You were interested, weren't you?'

'Yes, I was,' I said. 'Who killed Mopsy?'

'I did,' said Elspeth. 'And I've said I'm sorry, Melanie, but you know I don't approve of domestic pets.'

'And then I dropped off the parcel,' said Melanie, and took a deep pull at her joint. Her short skirt was up around her waist. She wasn't wearing stockings and suspenders. She was wearing black tights.

'And Grace helped me with the break-in at Melanie's,' said Elspeth. 'Because we're sisters.'

'We're sisters,' said Melanie. 'Grace?'

'We're sisters,' said Grace. The chuckle was back, but I could hear a note of self-deprecating irony in it, too.

'Any more claret?' said Nigel.

Melanie scrambled up and went to fetch him some. Elspeth explained to me, 'Melanie loves Nigel. So we all love Nigel. It's all right. Do you see, Alex? It's all right?'

'I see,' I said.

'And you must love Nigel too.'

'Right,' I said.

'Say it. Say "I love Nigel." '

'I love Nigel,' I said.

'Good for you,' said Barty, under his breath, and well under John Lennon, who was urging us to give peace a chance.

'How could you stand it?' I murmured.

'The Clinton option,' he said. 'I didn't inhale.'

Melanie, having opened the bottle for Nigel, sat down again, and Elspeth grasped her hand and Kate's. 'You see,' said Elspeth, 'we did it all for us. And you.'

'Who?' I said.

'From the beginning. Back then. To smash the glass ceiling. For the sisters. Us and those who would come after us. Kate and you and Nick. So it wouldn't be as bad for you,' said Elspeth. 'And it isn't, is it? Kate?'

'It's getting better,' said Kate.

'Alex?'

'It's much better,' I said.

'Nick?'

'I don't know what you mean,' said Nick.

Elspeth clapped. 'See? She doesn't even notice it. We've won.' She punched her fist in the air in a victory gesture.

'We've won,' said Melanie, also punching the air. 'Grace?'

'We've won,' said Grace, and raised her fist. That was the first time I've ever seen an ironic punch.

One of the Beatles was assuring us that he'd get high with a little help from his friends.

I took a joint from Barty and sucked it right down to my toes. The sixties were all that I had feared they would be.

Sunday, 3 October

Chapter 31

Peter woke me up at eleven. With the Sunday papers, flump on my stomach, and a retreating shout; 'Full fry-up on the table in fifteen minutes.'

When I'd washed and dressed and joined him, he looked neat. The beard had gone and he was wearing 'travel-for-work' clothes: clean jeans, black polo, leather jacket, desert boots. The Sammy boxes with his camera equipment were stacked near the kitchen door.

'Where are you off to?' I said.

'Thailand, I think. Or Singapore. It's on the ticket. Three weeks' work.'

'Nature doco?'

'Tragic treatment of Our British Prisoners in Fiendish Eastern Jail.'

'Oh. Good deal?'

'Not bad.'

That meant good. I was pleased for him. I'd almost miss him, I thought, as I looked out at the overcast sky and the drizzle. 'What's the weather like over there this time of year?' I said.

'No idea,' he said. 'I'll send you a postcard, let you know.' When we'd been together, all those years ago, I'd hovered in the hall morning after morning for the postman, waiting for Peter's scrawled cards, just in case he signed off 'love' instead of 'see ya' or 'take care'. Now, it didn't matter.

'That's the ceiling,' I said. 'But it isn't glass. It's — hormonal.'

'One sausage or two?'

'Two.'

'What d'you mean about the ceiling?'

'That's what keeps women . . . not down, so much as apart. The way their emotions bleed into everything. They take it personally.'

'Are you still in shock?'

'No.'

'So I'm supposed to say something intelligent back?'

'I'd settle for rational,' I said.

'I like that in women,' he said. 'They care about things, so I can, without feeling a berk. And they notice things, and do things, that I wouldn't think of. But that's what I remember about them. Like the way you used to push my hair behind my ears after we'd made love.'

I'd forgotten I ever did that. 'It looked uncomfortable for you, straggling into your eyes.'

'It was. But I didn't know it, until you noticed. I do it myself, now.'

He was eating. I couldn't, yet. I was still thinking. 'And the emotions go on, all mixed up. Which is why, I suppose, Elspeth killed the hamster. Because of the abortion. And why she killed the dog, too, in a way. She was angry. But she loves Melanie, too, and Melanie loves her, and Elspeth probably looked after Edward all those years for

Grace and Melanie, because Grace said after his first suicide attempt that he refused to see them. Elspeth was the only one he could bear to be with. Maybe because she was so insignificant, to him.'

Peter groaned. 'Is this a script conference for *Lezzy Loonies on the Job*?'

'No. It's about — sisters.'

'Sisters usually hate each other.'

'Only for a very small part of the time.'

'If you're not going to eat that, I will,' he said.

I stabbed his reaching hand with my fork. 'Get off, Barstow.'

He concentrated on his remaining food. 'D'you want to tell me what you're talking about?'

'Not really.'

'Where's O'Neill?'

'I left him behind in Oxfordshire, with all of them. They needed him. And Nick wanted to stay with Grace. And Nigel wouldn't go without Melanie. He thinks they're all mad, and he wants to keep her away from them. He doesn't like women together.'

'I'm with Nigel,' he said.

I looked at him. 'No, Peter,' I said. 'That's what I like about you. You're an unthinking, rugger-playing, supermasculine git, but you're not with Nigel. You never have been.'

After the taxi took him to Heathrow the flat seemed empty, and the next few hours — the rest of the day — stretched aridly in front of me.

I took the action list from the board, picked up the Arabella Trigg file, went through to the word-processor and loaded the disk. I could get the report done, at least.

I read Nick's shopping notes again. What would it be like, to be Arabella, to spend each morning choosing things? To play whatever shuffling game it was to avoid full disclosure in your accounts? What would it be like to have a husband who read your accounts? Was she going to tell him she'd paid the full price for the marked-down jacket, and that the underwear was from Harrods instead of Marks, and take the difference to pay her physiotherapist? So that she could stay perfect for him?

I tapped my fingers on the plastic of the keyboard. I could send Trigg the report he'd asked for. On the other hand, I could be a sister and give Arabella a ring, tomorrow, while he was at the office, and between us we could cook up a report she knew about and could substantiate, which left out unpleasant realities like incontinence. A wrenched shoulder, perhaps.

We'd manage it, easily enough, between us.

I replaced the notes in the file and put it aside.

The telephone rang.

'Alex Tanner.'
'This is Kinross. Is the boy there?'
'The boy?'
'Your boy. Nick. I need to speak to him.'

'I'll get Nick to ring you back.'

'When?'

'I'm not sure.'

'This is most inconvenient.' He sounded compos, sober and irascible. It took a while to get rid of him. For the last minute of our conversation I could hear a taxi throbbing outside, then pulling away.

When I rang off I went straight to the window. It was Barty, with a bulky parcel, about a metre and a half square and thirty centimetres deep. I chucked him the keys.

'Hi,' he said, lugging the parcel inside the door and propping it against the wall. 'Present from Grace.'

'Do you know what it is?'

'It feels like a picture,' he said, 'but I've no idea what of. When we all moved back to Grace's Hampstead place, Grace and Nick and Elspeth wrapped it up, with much giggling. They wouldn't let me see.'

'How are they?'

'Who in particular?'

'Elspeth and Melanie.'

'All right, for the moment. Melanie will survive it better than you think. She's never really liked Teddy.'

'Why?'

'I don't think she likes men, much.'

'What about Elspeth?'

'Grace will look after her. Are you going to give me a cup of coffee?'

I looked at Grace's present. 'No,' I said. 'Not now . . . I've things to do. Thanks for lending me the car last night.' I tossed him the keys.

He caught them. 'Oh,' he said. He looked surprised, and disappointed.

'Would you take me out to dinner?'

He perked up. 'Tonight?'

'Yep.'

'Where?'

'Somewhere smart. Somewhere crowded. Surprise me.'

'Right,' he said. 'I'll pick you up at half past seven.'

This time, when the door shut behind him, the flat wasn't empty. It was comforting. It was my own place, where I'd potter about with no clothes on, and play the Eagles, and dream. I'd go downstairs and ransack Polly's wardrobe, and come back up again and have a bath and shave my legs and pluck my eyebrows and do my face and hair.

Then I'd dress.

Then I'd look at myself in Grace's magic mirror.

The cheese-plant could whistle for a drink tonight; I'd get by, with a little help from my friends.

Tomorrow I'd take back the mirror. She needed it more than I did.

I'd have the last chuckle. Maybe not now, not even soon, but some time.

Because in 1969 I was five.

290